The Lament of Rebecca Downing

Gillian Wright

 New Generation Publishing

PART 1

ELIZABETH'S STORY

CHAPTER I

The journey to Heavytree to watch her daughter Rebecca die had been a long and arduous one. Elizabeth had walked most of the way, three days and nights. She had been passed by pack horses laden with fish, wool, and produce for the towns from the fishing villages dotted along coast, or returning with cloth, coal and kitchen ware and with sometimes pieces of lace and leather shoes for the well to do, but Elizabeth had not noticed as she trudged the lanes and tracks. Some of the lanes had been dark with overhanging trees, which, when meeting in the middle had created strange light patterns during the days, and an atmosphere of gloom during the nights. Occasionally she had walked along the beaches, her footprints making an impression on the damp sand for a short minute then disappearing, like Rebecca's short life. Memories flooded back as she walked these tracks and footpaths, rutted and treacherous. Once she had been able to hitch a ride from a rare passing cart, but on the whole walking had been her only form of transport. She might have taken a boat from Kingsbridge or Salcombe, up the coast, but that was too expensive. Some had tried to engage her in conversation, enquiring where she was going as she carried her small bundle containing some bread and cheese and the small amount of money she had saved, but were unable to do so, thinking her either standoffish or simple when she refused and just nodded her head as she passed on. How could it have come to this, she wondered. It was 1782 and men were boasting of an enlightened attitude towards others. Where was this evident in the case of her daughter?

Guilt flooded Elizabeth's consciousness, guilt of abandonment. The only child she had, and she had given her over to another to care for, denying her responsibility to this other human being she had brought innocent into the world. More obsessed with her position in the small village, having been already branded the daughter of a harlot and loose women by the others. Then finding herself in the same position as her mother with her pregnancy an abomination rather than a delight, she had been only too happy to relinquish the child and move on. On to another village, far away, where she would not be known, content to live the life of a servant until the rumours started to infiltrate her quiet existence. Rumours about a young apprentice girl from East Portlemouth who had murdered her master.

East Portlemouth, the name still brought bile to Elizabeth's throat. It had once been her village, a small village lying on the Salcombe estuary in rural south Devon, with farming and fishing the main industries, surrounded by the rolling hills and valleys of the South Hams. The village had been the property of the Duchess of Cleveland. A landlord she had never seen but had heard her name mentioned on occasions in hushed tones by the tenant farmers, villagers and the village poor, all reliant on this woman's goodwill. All she knew was that virtually all the property in the village, including her family's pathetic hovel of a home, belonged to her. Rent was due each month, and was met with great difficulty. The day the factor came round to collect the rents was always a frightening one, all the children of the village were told to be on their best behaviour, and keep out of site. Her grand-mother, Rebeccah, with whom she and her mother had lived, had worried every day of her life, and worked, along with the other women of the family to meet this deadline, otherwise they would be evicted to become vagrants and wanderers, usually to end up in the courts accused of being homeless and then thrown into the dreaded poorhouse.

Elizabeth's family, poor and generally nearly starving, were part of the bottom strata of the village, the 'undeserving poor'! She knew they were on the parish poor lists, living off the charity of the others, a liability and an expense to the village in general, and despised by those who could maintain themselves. Her only way out, marriage, but she had never been a respectable wife. Marriage had passed her by and at the age of 35 she was still a spinster. Who would have her in any case, the base-born daughter of her mother, also named Elizabeth , who, like Elizabeth herself, had been apprenticed to the Crispins, who had never been married but had other illegitimate children besides Elizabeth, farmed up at Rickham, about 2 miles away, when they both reached the age of ten years old.

One thing had been lacking in Elizabeth's life, one thing she had yearned for, but had never happened. A proposal of marriage. She knew how the village regarded her, a poor spinster, born out of wedlock, no beauty and with no hope. She had had the odd flirtation in her youth, but had never been bedded. At least not until that day up at Rickham, when she, at twenty years of age, who had never had any expectations of happiness, had suddenly realised what life could be and leapt the void into hope. Her heart had moved, and how she had paid for it, she and Rebecca. This 'transient connection' driven by 'appetite rather than affection' was how her love would be described in history, but she was not to know that. That was still to come.

Home in East Portlemouth had been a hovel in the Simples, the row of single story one-roomed cottages which lead from the heart of the village, high up on the

7

hill, down a narrow path through the valley to Simples beach, a small cove where the fishing boats were sometimes kept. Elizabeth lived with her mother, her grand-mother Rebeccah. They were crammed into the small living space which served as kitchen, living room and bedroom to all of them. Her life in the cottage was very hard. The pathetic hovel could barely keep out the weather, either in the cold wet freezing winters or the hot fly-ridden summers. They all lived in the one small room with a hearth and chimney large enough for a chimney seat on one side, for the use of her grand-father only as master of the house, and an oven on the other, with a round cast-iron pot and a trivet to hold the kettle, and a baking iron and bellows. The walls were of earth, under a low thatched roof, which if it rained, leaked regularly through onto the earthen floor making it damp and slippery: until the thatcher came to the village again, and only if her grandfather had any money, to repair the thatch as best he could. There was one straw stuffed mattress on a raised wooden platform in the corner which served as her grand-father and grand-mother's bed, with at intervals straw baskets for the new-born babies alongside. As the children grew, a talfat, a stage of boards placed immediately under the roof extending over half the living room with a railing, had been constructed which served for all them as a bed, with straw under old clothes as the mattress, with the leaking roof more often than not dripping onto the mattress rendering it permanently damp. How vividly she remembered never being dry, always cold in the winter, and often waking up to her clothes being frozen in the early morning. A dung pit, which served as an outside lavatory was situated just outside the cottage, which was never emptied but festered away, frozen in winter and stinking in summer. Cold water had to be fetched from the village pump every morning and

8

heated up over the fire, (that had been her job together with one of her brothers) but washing,(again her job with one of her sisters) what little was done, was outside whatever the weather. What clothes they had were mostly cast-offs from charity. Her brothers had worn breeches and smocks, for herself and her sisters smocks and petticoats. These had been made from home-spun material in the cottages of the better off who had spinning wheels, and then sewn by journeymen who travelled from village to village and house to house with their apprentices. These were usually in tatters and repaired by her grand-mother for Elizabeth and her siblings. Occasionally there were scraps of left- over material which her grand-mother made jackets from, and even more occasionally there were shoes, or wooden clogs, as she remembered. Food was scarce and nothing could not be eaten! Some barley, boiled in water with the liquid drained off served regularly as breakfast with a hunk of bread, lunch was usually a form of vegetable stew with the barley from breakfast, and with the occasional scrap of meat floating round, and for supper, bread and milk. Turnips and potatoes, leeks and pepper grass rolled up in a barley crust and baked in the ashes with a little milk made into a pastie was usual fare for her grand-father during the week, labourer food, but not for the young children, only for the boys if they were going to work in the fields. If her grand-mother had had a good week selling her remedies, on Sunday there would be a piece of mutton, roasted in the communal oven in the village, with potatoes. What heaven that had been! And always cider or ale for her grand-father, he never went without and always had the lion's share of everything. As children they really only got the scraps. How she had envied the children of the better off, with clothes that weren't rags and a Sunday best that they could go to Sunday school in, and more often than not full bellies. She had not even been able to go to Sunday school let alone proper school because she did not have a proper set of Sunday best clothes to go in.

When it became obvious that her mother had fallen pregnant out of wedlock when she was 17yrs old, she had been sent home by Ms Crispin, the farmer's wife where she had been apprenticed, back to live with her parents. Her grandfather had grudgingly agreed to take her back in. He, who was more often than not out of work and permanently on the parish poor list, received money from the parish poor fund on a regular basis to feed his family plus now his daughter's bastard. She had gone on to have three more. Occasionally he would be employed to work up at the church, or during harvest time at one or other of the farms. Sometimes he had work on one of the fishing boats, as most tenant farmers augmented their incomes by fishing. Elizabeth had been the product of a union, (as it was later to be described in the pamphlets printed after Rebecca's execution, and what a grand description for a short violent act up against a tree in the woods down Simples Lane, she thought!) between her mother and a jobbing farm labourer up at Rickham. Her mother and her bastard were tarnished and unmarriageable, but her grand- father, persuaded by his wife, her wonderful grand-mother had given them a roof over their head, and had agreed to look after her and her mother, provided they worked to supplement the meagre income and charity payouts the family lived on. And toil they did, working in the fields during harvest time whenever possible, or selling potions and remedies made from the herbs they had gathered and brewed up on instructions from her grand-mother, or else they were both beaten by her grandfather, Old John, a man with a short temper and a long arm!

Elizabeth's grand-mother Rebeccah had come from a long line of women healers and midwives. Once known as wise-women, they were often maligned as witches. The others in the village had thought of her grand-mother as such, like the witch of medieval times, who, by means of spells, charms and incantations could heal the sick, make barren women fertile, bewitch cattle, and who would have, one hundred years ago, and if she fell foul of the local population, end up at best on the ducking stool, at worst hanging from the nearest gallows. Still though, in small remote villages, women relied on other women who had knowledge of herbs and their medicinal properties for the care of the sick and the poor, those who were with child, those who could not conceive and those who were desperate not to become pregnant, or if pregnant with an unwelcome addition to the family to feed, to rid themselves of the child. In most country villages like East Portlemouth there could still be found a 'wise woman' like her grandmother, an expert in the practice of medicine, birthing and birth control. The poor of the village were able to afford these remedies, even though they could not afford the new male physicians and doctors who had become so fashionable and popular with the rich. Elizabeth's grandmother was much respected by the female population of the village as she had dispensed her herbal cures, looked after the sick, attended births, and coped with the alarm that ensued when someone found herself pregnant yet again with no money to feed the existing family let alone another mouth, and in desperation sought a way out. Elizabeth had had hopes of becoming as respected as her grand-mother, trying to remember all the potions and herbs and plants that she helped collect, until her plans had been ruined by her own unwanted pregnancy!

The tiny kitchen and herb garden behind her

grandfather's house had been her grandmother's responsibility and pride and joy, and was not only planted with vegetables, but contained the herbs which were essential for survival. Distilling homemade medicines had been part of daily life. Elizabeth's grandmother had understood the virtues and uses for these herbs. This knowledge had been passed down from her great-grandmother, and her female relatives before that . However the gathering of wild herbs was Elizabeth and her mother's job. These wild herbs were thought to be far more reliable and potent than the cultivated ones, particularly in the remedies for unwanted pregnancies. She understood from her grand-mother's teachings what to do with herbs such as Penny Royal, Motherwort, Parsley, Sage and Queen Anne's Lace. As a small girl, before she was sent away, she had been sent to the hedgerows and meadows to collect such herbs for her grandmother who would make the potions, and of course there was the Savin Juniper tree in Elizabeth's grandmother's garden, tucked in the corner, whose young shoots could be relied upon to bring about a late abortion. Many of her friends had made use of her grandmother's expertise, but not her mother nor indeed herself. Her mother had perhaps not realised she was pregnant till too late. She may indeed have tried grandmother Rebeccah's remedies. They were not guaranteed to work if the pregnancy was well advanced. She, Elizabeth, had not thought she had needed to either, at least not till it was too late.

He had said he would marry her, hadn't he? He had said he loved her and if she offered him her body he would stay with her for life. He had been so attentive that summer, telling her she was beautiful, something she had never heard before. The 'ugly one' was the way she was referred to by her mother's sisters and

12

brothers and her cousins. Not only ugly but base-born. What chance did she have of capturing a husband. She, Elizabeth, would show them. She would have a husband, and he would love her and the babe and cherish them just as he had promised. How wrong she was, and what a mess she had made of both her and her daughter's life.

CHAPTER II

Elizabeth sat down by the hedgerow for a minute while along her journey, dreaming of his face, his body and his hands. If she shut her eyes she could still smell him all those years after. Rebecca, the name she had given to her daughter, after her grandmother, had had a look of him when she was born. The stocky little body and blue eyes, the same mousy hair and ruddy skin. Maybe that was why she had found it easy to walk away, giving up her child to some-one else to rear, because she could not bare the reminder. He had left her but only after her body had swelled so much that she was of no more interest to him. Having promised marriage he had disappeared one day, never to be seen again; probably not for the first time he had moved on leaving destruction in his wake. She had tried to find him, asking passing strangers if they knew his whereabouts. And all the time she kept on working still at Rickham, cleaning the stables, picking up stones in the fields, collecting the cattle from the far pastures in all weathers, until her mistress had noticed her thickening waste and her breathlessness. Within a matter of hours she had been quizzed and dismissed, sent home once more to the hovel and her family, now without her mother, who had died two years previously, and her grandmother who had died a number of years before that; and there was no welcome there either.

Back in the small village those that were on the poor list and those that contributed to it defined their place in the village hierarchy, and it was a division which seemed unassailable. Elizabeth's family had been on the poor list ever since she could remember. Even while grandmother Rebeccah was respected, Old John, her grandfather, a lazy, drunken and ignorant man, had regularly been out of work and drunk what money he did earn. He claimed his poor relief every month, and the amount grew with the ever growing family. He was unworried with the stigma of being on the poor list and didn't seem to care or notice how it tarnished the whole of his family. He cared little for any of his surviving children, let alone bastard grandchildren, so Elisabeth, returning dismissed and pregnant, as her mother had done before her, could expect no truck from him when she arrived back.

Her grandfather, noticing her bulging shape as she stooped to go into the small cottage, had ranted and raged. It had been bad enough that her mother had had her, a base-born child, shaming the family, he had said. No-one blamed the man; in the late eighteenth century fornication was a woman's crime! She, Elizabeth, had been apprenticed away in order to remove her from his sight and his purse. Not that he really had one, she was quick to remember, depending on the hand-outs he received on a monthly basis from the church wardens. From the time of his marriage, five shillings per month was his payment, not a fortune, in fact barely enough to feed himself and his wife, let alone all the children. She had loved her grandmother Rebeccah, who had died 17 years before, finally worn out from child-bearing and the drudgery of a life of poverty. A life of trying to feed and clothe an ever growing family, afraid to use her own potions to prevent her regular pregnancies in case she was accused of murder by those in the village who had a grudge to bear, and relying on the barter gained from her medicines to supplement the family's starvation rations.

Elizabeth was starting to show her expanding waistline even under the serge shifts she wore, and life returned to the dreadful drudgery she had remembered. Life up at Rickham had in reality been a welcome relief. There had always been food on the table, clean clothes, and occasionally a word of encouragement from her mistress. She had been aware that she was one of the lucky ones. Other pauper children from the village were sent as apprentices far away, some to work in the towns and mills of the north and had never come back. Gossip recounted the deaths of a few, either from abuse or starvation. The one thing she had to be grateful for was that her mother had never abandoned her to a parish nurse to be wet-nursed and cared for in her early years.

Parish nurses who were paid to foster infants in their own homes were sometimes known as 'killing nurses' because so few of their charges survived! Elizabeth's mother had withstood all the beatings and bullying from her father, and with grandmother Rebeccah's support, had managed to keep young Elizabeth at her side, working as often as she could after the baby was born, leaving her in the care of her grandmother. Working in the houses of the wealthy of the village, like the Jarvis family. Jonathon Jarvis was a church warden as was his brother Richard. Both were a tenant farmers in East Portlemouth, but Richard had become an early widower, his wife, daughter and her husband having died of typhoid, as did many during the epidemics that occurred with monotonous regularity.

****

Elizabeth now knew that her daughter Rebecca had been apprenticed to this Richard Jarvis by the parish when she had reached the age of eight. From passing gossip, from the tinkers who moved through the small villages in the county selling their wares, she had learnt that he had a reputation for violence, but she had buried that at the back of her mind.

Her mother had even been back to Mrs Crispin up at

Rickham, after Elizabeth was weaned, to work again, and was able to send money back to appease Old John. Now what could she, Elizabeth, do, with her mother and grandmother both dead. She could not stand up to her grand-father. She would not find work with a baby at her side. She would have to abandon the child, find work elsewhere and hope that it would be cared for.

She had gone into labour suddenly, whilst in the fields searching for the herbs that she had been taught about by her mother. She had been making medicines secretly, selling them in the village, potions to make a man fall in love with you, potions to stop pregnancy, a very dangerous thing to do she knew, in order to give Old John money to prevent the beatings. She had received a severe one that morning, maybe, she thought, that was why the pains had started. She was not due for another three weeks by her calculations, and every-one knew if you had only been with a man once, when your baby would come. No expensive mid-wife for her, her only hope was to get back and call for a neighbour to help. The miseries that some women had endured, and she had seen, when an unskilled midwife was all that was available, were too horrible to contemplate. Elisabeth hoped against hope that Joan Hutchings, the most skilled in the village, would be there to help. Joan was no midwife like old Rebeccah, but at least she had assisted on occasions in the village and had taken over old Rebeccah's role as village midwife after her death. The risk of Elisabeth's child being still born or dead within a day of life was high, as was the risk of her dying in childbirth. [1] Maybe, she mused, it would have been better if either of those awful occurrences had happened.

As she had stumbled down the lane to her cottage,

---

[1] See Notes at back

crying out as she went to her neighbours, she had felt the wetness between her legs. The pains had increased in strength and by the time she reached her door they were coming almost every five minutes. Fortunately her grand-father, Old John, had been away, for once working out at the Jarvis farm as it was July and there was a harvest to get in, and not likely to be back till late that evening. Elizabeth had sat on the chair, bent double, waiting for help to come. A figure had appeared in the doorway, casting a long shadow into the room, it was Joan Hutchings. Moving her to the trestle bed in the corner, firstly removing the filthy sheets that Old John had used for the last year, he being the only one allowed a bed whilst the others slept on straw pallets covered with blankets on the floor or on the telfat. Joan, snorting with disgust as she did so, had pulled out from her basket a sheet, crumpled but clean, and laid it on the bed. Pulling Elizabeth from the chair she had moved her onto the bed. In the meantime another neighbour had appeared at the door carrying a pot of hot water and some cloths. Joan had instructed her to fetch some wood and light the fire in the small grate. This she did and placed an old copper kettle full of water over the flames. The bearing pains were coming at shorter intervals and Elisabeth, lying back on the bed, had started to moan. She had been in attendance with Joan at a number of births and was aware of the procedure. Other women from the village had joined Joan, having been summoned to help. This summoning of the women signalled the imminence of the birth. Elizabeth had heard her mutter to the other women as she knelt down in front of her that the 'presentation' was normal, no complications, and she was relieved. She had seen women die in childbirth due to complications during the time she had been up at Rickham. Giving birth was a dangerous business.

After what seemed like a lifetime, but in fact was only a matter of hours, she had given birth. Joan had severed the umbilical cord, tying it with string and washed and wrapped the little body in swaddling bandages, 'Yer are delivered of a girl, blessed be to God' she had told Elizabeth, and with that the baby had started crying. 'Here, yer better get on with it. What are yer going to name 'er?' she had said placing the infant in Elizabeth's arms. With that she had left the cottage accompanied by the others. There would be no celebration of this birth as there would have been had the child been legitimate and wanted. Elizabeth would not name the father either, as was sometimes done in front of witnesses by the mother of an illegitimate baby at the time of birth[2], and after they had gone had sat up, dropped the top of her shift and presented her breast. Milk was beginning to flow and the small mouth, searching blindly had eventually found the nipple. All had become quiet except the slight sound of her child suckling.

She must have fallen asleep with the baby tucked into the crook of her arm, but she had woken with a start as Old John appeared in the doorway. 'So it's done is it?' he had said. He had walked across the room, filthy from the fields. 'What is it then?' he had demanded, without looking at the child.

'A girl' she said.

'Well yer better get 'er christened.' And with that he had walked out of the cottage, down to the ale house. It was going to be a long night.

Chapter III

It had started to rain. Her journey continued and July could be changeable. Although it wasn't cold Elizabeth pulled her cloak tighter round her thin shoulders. One day and night had already passed, and she still had at least two days to go to get to Exeter. Panic set in as she hurried on. She had to be there to bear witness to this miscarriage of justice. Her daughter Rebecca, however much provoked, and she suspected Richard Jarvis of much cruelty, would not have had the intelligence to have done the deed. 'Rebecca were not quite right in the head' Elizabeth had been told by those that knew her and had passed on snippets of information whenever they had passed through the village where she had hidden herself away all those years.

Night started to set in; Elizabeth pulled a piece of bread from her bag and started to eat. She had managed to put together some food and money from her meagre wages, before she had left the village. Her present mistress of the last fourteen and a half years, the wife of a tenant farmer in the village of Halwell, near Totnes, some thirty miles north of East Portlemouth, a kind woman in spite of her rough manner, had listened to her story and allowed her to leave the farm and to leave her chores on the farm as well as the cleaning, mending and cooking, and tending to her mistress's sick husband with her herbal potions, for a week but no longer. She knew if she overstepped the mark her position as trusted house servant would be lost and she would be replaced. There were many waiting in the wings for employment such as hers. Good positions were hard to find and the last winter had been harsh. She knew that many in rural Devon had died from illness and starvation, brought on by disease and the bad harvest from the previous summer. She wondered how those in East Portlemouth had survived. Fishing and farming were the main providers of sustenance and both had suffered badly. She also wondered if Old John was still alive. He would be an old man, now in his seventies and probably more ill tempered than ever. He would be about the same age as Richard Jarvis had been before his death by poisoning. Arsenic so the doctor said, Rebecca could not read or write so how could she have known what was in the bottle, she wandered.

Her mind returned to Rebecca's birth. Old John had returned from the ale house later that night. She had heard him as he struggled to open the door, and stumbled to the bed. She had managed to leave it and was now lying on her pallet in the corner of the room, trying to keep the mewling baby from waking him as he snored his way through the rest of the night. The following morning she had woken , after snatched periods of sleep between feeding, to find him gone. She had risen and left the sleeping baby on the pallet as she attempted to tidy up the room, removing the blood covered sheet that she had given birth on, and he had slept on in his drunken stupor, and had replaced the old one back on the bed. She had taken a bucket to the stand pipe in the village, with the baby strapped to her front in a sling, to draw water, then returned to the cottage. She had slowly washed the grumbling infant and marvelled at the baby's small limbs. Putting her to her breast she had sat quietly while the baby suckled. Rebecca, that is what she would name her, she mused, after her much loved grandmother. Maybe her grandfather would be pleased by that and have a bit more patience with her? She had wondered how long it would be till he turned them out. She knew she would not be able to support herself or Rebecca if she had nowhere to live. The best she could hope for was to

21

throw herself on the mercy of the church wardens and find some-one to take the baby on, and let the church pay for her upkeep. She would go away and find work elsewhere and send money back. It would be impossible to find work with a child. Suddenly a thought had come to her. Joan Hutchins had looked after another bastard child in the village a few years ago, and she had just had a child of her own, one she and her husband, who was now dead, could barely afford. There was no parish nurse but Joan was the nearest to one. She now needed the money. Perhaps she could ask the wardens if they would pay Joan to look after Rebecca whilst she found work elsewhere. She couldn't wait to get away as the realisation of her position hit her. A bastard of a bastard with a bastard! A parish nurse could receive good money; she knew Joan had received five shillings per month for the last baby she took in. That was the answer she had decided, and the sense that she was abandoning her child was pushed to the far recesses of her mind.

Elizabeth had swaddled the baby once more in its bandages, fed her and had hurried out of the cottage up the valley to the church overseer's house. She knew she had to make her move now. She had climbed the hill up to the top where she could see the ancient Norman church of St Winwalloe as she reached the end of the path. Jonathon Jarvis, one of the powerful Jarvis family and a tenant farmer of substance, was overseer, and responsible for the parish poor of East Portlemouth. He was usually in the church every early morning. She had struggled on up the hill, tired and weary from delivering the day before, and walked under the latch gate and along the path to the door of the church. As she had looked down at the sleeping babe a moment of emotion had flooded through her. Could she do this? If only she could write a note, but the frustration of illiteracy, she could neither read nor write because it was not considered important for a pauper girl child such as herself to be educated so she had never attended the village school, had made her hesitate. She wanted to run away and leave the baby in the porch, but by now she had realised that everyone knew the child was hers and would search for her. Joan and the other women would have seen to that. As she had hesitated Jonathon Jarvis came through the church door, a tall forbidding man, thin and angular, dressed in black breeches, frock coat and hat. Elizabeth had flung herself on the ground in front of him with the baby bobbing and yelling all at the same time, and had prevented him from walking by. He had looked down, and put out a hand to help her up.

'What is it Elizabeth?' he had asked. He was a kindly man, so different from his brother Richard.

'Please look after moi child.' She had muttered. 'Oi'll go and look for work and send money back when Oi can'. Aware, as he was as overseer of the village poor, that the child was in reality already a burden on the tax payers of the village, and that if Elizabeth left it would be one less mouth to feed, he had quickly realised that, though he would have to pay some-one to look after the child, it would be cheaper than keeping them both in the village. If Elizabeth did send money back then that would be even better.

'Joan Hutchins 'as taken in children 'efore'. She had said. 'Then sh'll be apprenticed and no longer a burden to yer and O'ill continue to send money ter repay the village.'

'I will have to consult with the other wardens, and will inform you shortly'. He had said. 'Now go home and look after your baby for the moment'. He had turned and walked towards Higher Farm where he was the tenant farmer, a man of substance on the biggest farm in the neighbourhood.

'I will call a meeting tonight', he had announced over his shoulder, 'and give you the verdict tomorrow'.

She had gathered Rebecca into her arms and had walked slowly back down the valley. As she had reached the cottage she heard her grand-father's voice coming from inside. Horrified, she had wandered where to flee to. But before she could he had appeared at the door.

'Well whore, don't think yer can stay 'ere with that bastard of yers. Oive had enough of bastards in this family. Yer can pack yer bags and go, with yer brat.' he had drunkenly shouted. She had faced him, quaking and waiting for him to lift his fist.

'I will leave tomorrer. I must arrange for her to be christened first' she had said. Elisabeth prayed silently that Jonathon Jarvis could persuade the wardens. Then she had had a thought. If she abandoned the baby they would have no alternative but to look after her. The law said so! She would leave during the night. She would put Rebecca on Joan's doorstep. She knew that Joan would take the child in if she heard her cry. They would look for her, but by then she would be long gone, out of the parish to the north. She still had her apprenticeship papers. She would not go as a vagrant for then she would be imprisoned, but as a servant, with references. She was quick witted and hard-working. And then she would send money back and they would forgive her. Maybe one day she could even come back and see her daughter, thriving and growing up?

Chapter IV

Elizabeth woke up on the second morning of her journey with a sense of dread. Following the map she had been given of her journey which would take in many towns and villages, both down unmade country lanes designed for foot or horseback travellers and then on to main thoroughfares, used by carts and coaches, she realised she had to hurry or else she would not have the time to see Rebecca before her execution! This map, given to her by her mistress, and made small enough to fit into backpacks and saddle bags, showed roads, bridges, rivers, woods, fields, private lands, and landmarks and obstacles to be encountered along the way from town to town. Many of the towns beyond Halwell she had heard of but never visited. Totnes was the farthest she had ever been, to the market and to the annual fare. The map guided her onwards to Ipplepen, Newton Abbott, across to Teignmouth, and up along the coast to Dawlish. These roads were main thoroughfares, taking the carts and pack horse trains and the odd coach to Exeter. Exeter was a big county town, the centre of the serge industry; this was where the cloth was made to make up the heavy army coats, breeches, and even the cloak she was wearing. She had seen the fleeces washed and sorted, carded and combed to form lengths of fibre which were spun by the women in the village cottages of Halwell to make the yarn that formed serge. This yarn was then taken from all parts of Devon to Exeter to be woven by the local serge weavers, well paid at nine shillings a week, nearly ten times the poor money she and her family had to live on. Her serge cloak was a throw-out from her mistress, a dirty blue in colour, given to her by her mistress shortly before she left, and another small kindness she remembered as she walked on. To be sure it rubbed her round her neck and shoulders, and was too big for her, her mistress was a large lady, but never-the less it kept the worst of the weather out.

She would need to pay a toll at instances along these roads. She had counted her money carefully before leaving, she had five pounds, she hoped fervently that this amount was enough to get her through and to pay for lodgings in Heavitree and the forthcoming bribes! From Dawlish she would need to head inland on the farm tracks and paths to Kenton, then Exminster and up to Countess Wear.

As Elizabeth walked the road to Exeter from Countess Wear she noticed a sign post to Liverydole and her heart lurched. Tomorrow her daughter would be dragged by horse on a sledge to the area known as Liverydole in Ringwell, two miles outside the city, where the public executions took place, from the prison set in the city's South Gate. Elizabeth had heard that conditions at Exeter prison were notoriously bad, with condemned prisoners kept chained in small underground cells, dank dark and infested with rats, with no light, and vermin and insects crawling everywhere. With no ventilation either they would be suffocating in the summer heat of July. She knew they were given very little water, and what was given was stale and foul. She had heard how prisoners fought with the rats for mouldy bread and scraps and many starved to death before their sentences were being carried out. Women gave birth to babies who were left to die on the piles of filthy straw, and fellow prisoners suffering from goal fever, a virulent form of typhus, died with regularity. Here the debtors ward was called the 'shew' because the inmates begged for food by letting down a shoe from the window to beg from passers by. It was widely known that more prisoners died from the conditions in the prison than ever reached trial or sentence. The only small consolation was that she knew that Rebecca had only been there for a short time, less than a few months since her conviction, and had been held in a ward prior to that before she stood trial, and then held for about a month in the condemned cell before she was convicted, and amazingly she had survived that ordeal.

Elizabeth knew that along the three miles to the place of execution the procession would be followed by large crowds all the way. She only hoped that Rebecca would be too dazed to hear the jeering and shouting, too dazed to feel the hurled stones and other missiles that would follow her to her death. She hoped that the jailer could be bribed to arrange for her to have some strong ale or gin before she was chained to the horse drawn sledge, to numb her brain sufficiently and deaden the panic and fear that she would inevitably feel. She had been told that the prison jailers and keepers derived part of their large profits from the sale of alcohol, so she was hopeful her offer of money would be accepted. This was the reason for hurrying. The small amount of money she carried was earmarked for bribing the executioner as well. She had been told it would be possible, if she got there early enough and with enough money, she might also be able not only to see her daughter but speak with her jailer. And finally she needed to bribe the executioner to make sure Rebecca was dead, garrotted, before the faggots were lit.

She smelt Exeter before she reached the bustling town. Across the meadows and fields that surrounded the outskirts, with their slums and shambles, the place of the butchers for slaughtering their meat for sale in the markets, came the smell of dead flesh, sewerage and general living together in confined spaces, tempered by the salt smell of the sea and the rank smell of the river mud. She held her nose for a while until she got used to it, gagging at the first heady rush. The day was already warm and she untied the strings of her cloak. At least, she mused, her shoes would dry in the sun today as she walked, instead of slurping along in the rain as they had for the past few days. She was starting to feel sick. Worry and concern for Rebecca flooded her mind, together with the very obvious thought that maybe her child might not recognise her. After all she had not had any contact for the last fifteen years.

Rebecca had been a new-born babe when Elizabeth had left her on Joan Hutching's doorstep that afternoon, and even though there had been the occasional money she had sent to the parish for Rebecca's keep there had been no contact during those years between mother and child. She did not know even if her child knew she was alive still. She had escaped the wrath of her grandfather and the shame of her position, but not without a second thought. She had had many thoughts that day as she ran from the village with her few belongings and her apprentice papers which she had been able to find in the cottage, clutched to her. Terrible feelings of regret and loss coupled with the need to escape had overwhelmed her. She had travelled along the paths north not knowing where she was going. She had had wanted to try to reach Totnes. She had once been taken there to the annual fare, a childish treat, and one of the very few she had ever received. She had been taken by her grandmother in a hired cart driven by a hired cart-man. She was not sure why her grandmother had needed to go to Totnes, but she remembered hushed discussions around the lack of certain herbs, and the need for one particular herb, to be purchased as soon as possible and taken back to the village, but for whom she had no idea. Totnes had been exciting. It had a castle and it even had a leper walk outside the walls on the outskirts of the bustling hill-top town, with holes in it through which the lepers could put their hands to receive alms and food from the wary town dwellers, who would not want to catch the dreaded disease, or see the ravages it caused. She remembered the steep walk up the narrow centre of the town, and the bridge across leading from the town prison, where Rebecca would have been taken the first day on her way to Exeter for her trial. She remembered the market held a little further up in the town square where farmers from the surrounding villages had bought their goods to sell. It was there that her grandmother had taken her, dragging her up the hill so fast that her small feet had barely touched the ground and she had had very little time to take in the sights and smells. It was to one of the stalls that they had rushed. Her grandmother had produced from her purse discreetly hidden under her long skirt, a few coins, and after whispered words, the old crone behind the stall had disappeared for a few minutes, to come back with a small brown piece of paper wrapping what appeared to be something spiky and stick like. Elizabeth was to learn later that this was Myrrh, a rare and valued plant from the East. The gum extracted from this expensive plant was known to be, when added to certain other herbs, the strongest abortifacient known. This, she had guessed, had to be for some-one very rich and very desperate, who could afford the most expensive. Her grandmother was taking an enormous risk collecting this plant and if found using and dispensing it could face being charged with murder and hung. Elizabeth never did know who this person was. It had been a darkly kept secret in the village. Her grandmother had never divulged the secret, and indeed she did not even know if the remedy had worked. But Totnes had remained a fascination to her, not only because of the lepers but because it was the place of secret and dangerous things.

CHAPTER V

This was all in the past. It was now dusk and she had to hurry on. In 1782 Exeter was still an ancient city and had been slow in adopting the modern improvements. There were virtually no pavements and no cleaning of streets so it still had the unsavoury odour of a medieval town. One great street ran through the city from East to West. Only this main street was lit by gas and had pavements. The rest consisted of dirty, pot-holed lanes, airless and unlit, where the majority of the inhabitants lived at bare subsistence level. To be sure there were rich prosperous merchants but they lived in their newly constructed grand houses outside the city walls, well away from the 'common herd', the unsavoury smell and the squalor. Elizabeth was heading for the South Gate which served as the town prison. There she hoped to find some sort of lodging near by for the night. The next day she would try to see the prison warder. Passing along the narrow lanes with her head down, she hoped to find a friendly face to ask directions. The streets were still awash with people and animals. Pack horses were being led to their stables for the night by shouting grooms, beggars were beginning to move away to the outskirts of the city, for fear of being taken in for vagrancy, women were heading home to prepare the evening meal, carrying their provisions tightly clutched under their arms for fear of robbery. Children were running down the centre of the lanes, dodging the oncoming carts and the odd carriage, and pamphlet sellers were beginning to put away their pamphlets and stop shouting the news. It was the latter that caught her notice. She could not read, but she heard the seller repeat to a last minute purchaser, 'It's all here, execution at Heavitree the day after tomorrow. Read the full story here!'

She averted her eyes and hurried down towards the South Gate. She passed an ale-house, where the smell of filthy bodies and cheap perfume and thick tobacco wafted through the open door. Gin and ale were cheap, and an easy way to stem the hunger pains! A young woman lurched out of the door, struggling to keep her feet, badly in need of washing and with the hard hollow look of the street. Her once cream muslin dress, scooped low to expose as much of her breasts as possible, was soiled with past customers leavings, and her stomacher so filthy it wanted de-lousing.

'What yer looking at?' she snarled as she picked herself up from the muddy street. Elizabeth was close to tears and choked as she tried to reply. The woman, by then on her feet, looked closely at her.

'What yer cryin for, yer ain't got no reason, yer don't look 'ungry!' Elizabeth sank to her knees sobbing with great gulps of anguish, suddenly overcome - her grief and heartbreak all too obvious. The woman, surprising even herself, stopped in her tracks, and from somewhere deep down in her psyche she recognised this desperate anguish and a feeling for a fellow member of her sex swelled up and she felt compassion. 'Where are yer goin?' she asked,

'Oi don't know' Elizabeth replied in between sobs, 'Oi'm looking for somewhere to stay tonight and Oi've very little money.' The woman recognized the deep soft devon drawl, unlike her own harder mid-devon accent.

'Where yer from then?' she asked. Yer not from 'ere.'

'Oi'm from the south, a village called East Portlemouth.' For a moment the woman stood still, a blank look on her face, then all of a sudden recognition of the place name dawned. 'Oh my Gawd, the lass who's being burnt tomorrer, she come from that village.'

'She's moi daughter'. Elizabeth crumpled now in a heap on the dirty lane. The woman grabbed her arm and dragged her to her feet,

'Come with me, it ain't much but yer can lodge with me. Oi don't need any more genlemen tonight, but hurry, yer don't want them inside to know who yer are, they think yer daughter's a witch!' and with that she pulled Elizabeth along through narrow streets, down filthy paths until they came to a flight of steps. Elizabeth, blinded by her grief, had not noticed in which direction or where they had been going, nor had she been aware of her surroundings. 'Up 'ere' the woman had said, as she hauled her up the steps till they came to a small grubby door. Putting her finger against her lips and hissing 'Shhh!' they both tiptoed into the inner hall and up another flight of ill-lit greasy stairs until they were faced with a battered wooden door. The woman now retrieved a key from her grimy petticoats, and putting it in the lock, opened the door.

At first nothing was visible in the darkness of the tiny room. Only the outline of a small window at one end, so dirty virtually no light could force its way through the grime. The woman moved forwards after closing the door, and fumbled for a taper from her moth- eaten purse, then moved into the room, bent down to the floor and lit the remains of a small candle that was precariously balanced on a cracked saucer. The candlelight flickered and threw shadows round the tiny room. There was a truckle bed against one wall, covered with a ragged grey blanket of sorts and an old pillow. A chair was the only other piece of furniture in the room, covered in what at first sight appeared to be a pile of old rags, which suddenly moved!

'Get out of 'ere yer miserable sod,' the woman said, 'Oi told yer to be gone by the time Oi got back.' And

33

with that the pile of rags shuffled towards the door, muttering unintelligibly, opened it without a backwards glance, and left. Elizabeth stood bemused in the middle of the room. 'Oi ain't got no food, but if yer've got a couple of pennies Oi can go and get us a pie each, and a jar'. Elizabeth opened her purse and took out two of her precious pennies. She handed them over, not giving a thought to the fact that she might never see the woman again. The woman grabbed the money and walked out into the night.

Elizabeth moved towards the chair. Her life had been bad, but she had never had to whore for a living. For that she was thankful. She sat down and put her head into her hands. She did not know where she was in this large and unfriendly city. What could the woman have meant? Who thought Rebecca was a witch? What evil nonsense was this? It could not be the sentence of burning. In 18th century England witches were hung not burnt. Who had put this dreadful thought about? It could only have been someone from East Portlemouth. She remembered how on some occasions there had been whispers about her grandmother; vicious gossip in the village, that old Rebeccah could cast spells. She remembered her grandmother being very worried after they had collected the Myrrh from Totnes, and she remembered she had overheard conversations concerning the age of the 'girl' who had been treated by her grandmother. She remembered a visit from John Jarvis shortly before, and knew there had been some connection. She had heard the word 'witch' being cast about in the village, in hushed tones as she, or her grandmother went about their daily business. But nothing had come of it and the gossip had been put to rest. May-be this was why the trial had been so short, and the sentence so dreadful. Perhaps Rebecca had been also tainted by the reputation of her great grandmother but who could have influenced the judge and jury? Who could have wanted Rebecca out the way so quickly? Elizabeth sat, her mind churning, unaware of the time passing. Suddenly the door opened and the woman returned, clutching in her arms two pies and a bottle of gin. '

'Ere ye' are' she said, now tell me yer story.' She went to the corner of the bed and pulled a cracked glass out from under the mattress. She filled it to the brim with the gin and passed it to Elizabeth.

'Drink and yer'll feel better' she said.

Elizabeth woke the next morning, and for a moment couldn't think where she was. She had a headache tumbling round the back of her head and her eyes. She sat up and realised she was lying on the floor with her cloak wrapped round her. It was dawn and the light was attempting to come through the filthy window. She heard snoring coming from the bed above her and everything came flooding back. With horror she realised she had no idea where abouts in Exeter she was. She had to get to the prison to see the warder before it was too late. She had to see Rebecca and tell her she loved her and was sorry. Grabbing her cloak she got up, knocking the empty bottle of gin over as she did. Creeping to the door so as not to wake the snoring body, she carefully opened it, and slipped down the stairs and out of the building. The sun was beginning to rise above the buildings and narrow streets. She tripped over a beggar lying at the bottom of the steps, but he didn't move. She had to find her way to the South Gate. As she passed through a small square she saw a pillory in the middle, still surrounded by the rotting fruit, eggs, and stones that had been thrown at some poor wretch who had been imprisoned in the ghastly contraption previously. She passed a miserable thatched cottage located behind the Guildhall which

35

had a sign outside saying 'Exeter House of Correction'. She shuddered as she knew it was here that prisoners were held for short-term custodial sentences and petty crimes. The smell of stale sewage and bodies from the disgusting building permeated the morning air. She continued on realising she didn't even know the name of the woman who had helped her, and knowing she must ask her way from someone. She ran on until she came across a small boy hunched in the gutter. Asking him the way she was astonished by the look of horror that crossed his face as she mentioned the name of the prison.

'Yer be near the South Gate' he said as he wiped his hand across his knees, and then made the sign of the cross.

'Down there and keep straight on'. She hurried on down running as fast as she could till she finally saw ahead of her the prison door set in the side wall. Quivering inside she reached up to the rusty knocker and rapped on it twice. After what seemed an age a voice from behind the door shouted for her to give her business.

'Oi've come ter visit the prisoner Rebecca Downing', she managed to stammer out, 'Oi'm 'er mother.'

'Only just in time!' he growled, and this was followed by a hoarse laugh as the door began to open. The warder stood in front of her, an imposing man of average height but more than average width. His arms were huge and he held out his hand indicating that he required money, compensation for his time, before he would take her any further. Elizabeth reached inside her purse a brought out a shilling and gave it to him.

As the smell of human waste, sweat and filth and of fear permeated her nostrils, Elizabeth recoiled in horror. Reaching the inner part of the prison, through dark, damp corridors, musty and smelly in spite of the summer weather, she was lead down an ancient winding stone staircase, deeper and deeper into the depths. She followed the warder through the darkness. Occasionally she glimpsed, through the bars of the cells, and saw sickly bodies curled up against the walls of the small spaces they were confined in. At last he stopped in front of cell door at the bottom of this deep dark ghastly pit. Reaching for his bundle of keys he opened the door and stood aside for her to go in.

'Oi'l be back shortly' he growled.

CHAPTER VI

In the damp rank dusky cell Elizabeth could make out, huddled in the corner, rocking back and forth on her haunches, a beaten and bloody waif. Her clothes were torn and soiled and she smelled strongly of urine and faeces. Her face and hair was streaked with filth, and she had an open and bleeding wound on her forehead. Her legs were in iron shackles, attached in turn to an iron ring embedded in the dirty flag stone floor. Elizabeth turned to the warden,

'If Oi pay can yer remove 'er chains just while Oi'm 'ere?' she pleaded. He nodded as she passed over another shilling and he crouched down to unlock the irons. Rebecca did not move, just continued rocking and now moaning gently to herself. The warden turned and bade her shout if she needed assistance, then left and closed the door behind him and she heard the grating noise of the key turning the lock. Sobbing quietly to herself Elizabeth moved forward and knelt down in front of the rocking figure. She gently touched the girl's shoulder. The child recoiled and shrunk back in fear, looking up with terror.

'Why am Oi 'ere?' The choked words came from the chapped lips, and Elizabeth realised these were the first words she had ever heard her daughter say. And now they would probably be amongst the last!

She reached out again and took Rebecca's grimy hands into her own. 'Who are yer?' the child asked. Although she was fifteen by Elizabeth's reckoning, she was undersized and thin to the point of starvation.

'Oi'm yer mother.' Elizabeth sobbed.

'Oi don' have a mother.' was the reply. There was a blank stare on Rebecca's face. 'Oi don' have a father either, and Oi killed my master!' With that she started rocking again, back and forth whilst Elizabeth kept hold of her hands. Remorse, shame and guilt flooded Elizabeth's heart and mind.

'What's going to 'appen to me?' Rebecca asked, 'why am Oi 'ere?' she demanded again. Elizabeth tried to put her arms around her daughter to comfort her. Rebecca recoiled again. Once more a blank uncomprehending look came across her face.

'Are they going ter let me go tomorrer?' she asked. 'Oi should so like ter go 'ome'. Elizabeth realised that her daughter had not grasped the awful truth of her plight, that she was not aware what was going to happen to her tomorrow. Maybe it would be better not to tell her. Maybe, if she could bribe the warden to ply her with gin she would not realise what was happening to her.

'Yes, yer're going home tomorrow' she gently said, through sobs, 'Just close yer eyes all the way there and yer'ill reach home.'

'Who'm Oi going to work for as me master is dead?' Rebecca demanded, her face suddenly lighting up with the thought of her return. She struggled to get to her feet, but her knees buckled, unable to support her yet after the cramped position she had been in for the last couple of days after her trial. As she fell forward Elizabeth caught her in her arms. Holding the small body close she crooned to her gently.

'Oi'm so sorry my darlin' child.' she whispered, 'If only Oi 'ad been there ter take care of yer,' Rebecca's face remained blank. She stiffened and backed away from Elizabeth's arms.

''Ave yer got any food? She asked, 'Oi'm so 'ungry.' Elizabeth realised that the one thing she should have brought she did not have. Had she really expected her child, her baby, to know or acknowledge her after all these years. Of course she would have been told her mother had abandoned her, and perhaps even that she was dead. Rebecca looked at her,

'Go away'. she said, 'Oi don't know yer! Oi'm going home tomorrow any way so Oi'll get food then.'

There was a rattle of keys and the door opened. Rebecca shrunk back and sank to her knees.

'Well witch, ' the warder growled, 'time to put yer chains back on to make sure yer don't fly out the window 'efore tomorrow and yer big day!' He bent down and placed the fetters back around the child's thin chafed ankles. Rebecca started to rock again and did not look up as Elizabeth was pushed out the door of the cell, the warder locking it behind her.

'Oi should make yerself scarce before they call yer witch too' he laughed, as he pushed Elizabeth up the stairs and through the corridors until they finally reached the prison door. Elizabeth realised that it was now or never the time to try to bribe him to buy gin or ale for Rebecca and to make sure she had had enough to dull her mind to block out the ghastly journey she must take tomorrow. Could he be trusted? She had no alternative.

'Please Sir,' she said, 'She is moi daughter, she is only a child, moi only child, please, if Oi give yer money now, will yer give her enough gin or ale tomorrer ter help her through? Enough to dull her mind ter what's happening?' ''ow much have yer got?'

'Yer'll need to pay the executioner as well.' he replied. She reached once more into her purse and pulled out another shilling.

'Oi've only enough now for the executioner,' she said, praying that this amount would satisfy him.

'Well, we ain't seen a burning for some time, poor wretch,' he said, and took the money. 'Glad it ain't my daughter.' And with that he pushed her through the open prison door out on to the street once more.

Where should she go now? She had to make for

Heavitree before the crowds. Struggling to come to terms with the awfulness of what she had just witnessed, and with her guilt and heartbreak, Elizabeth knew she had to be there tomorrow and close by in order to be able to beg and bribe the executioner to strangle Rebecca before the flames were lit. God knows she did not want to witness her daughter dying, but would God give her the strength to be there for her. She clutched her purse to her. In it were the six remaining shillings. She had no money for food or lodging, but she didn't care. As she walked on she passed a pamphlet seller, once more setting up to sell the days pamphlets. She could not read but she knew she had to have one, then, if she went in to the nearest church perhaps she could beg the priest to read it to her. This was the pamphlet that Elizabeth had seen for sale the previous day, and would purchase now. Later she would purchase the final account because on execution day or soon afterwards came the full broadsheet, embellished with accounts of the trial, confession and execution, verses, and sometimes woodcut portraits of the gallows scene.

Moving towards the boy, the same one she had noticed the evening before peddling these pieces of journalistic news, Elizabeth proffered a half penny, the going rate. He handed her a sheet covered in print. Frustrated by the fact she could not read any of it she noticed a church near-by and walked quickly inside, mindful that she had little time left to get to Heavitree before the crowds. Fortunately there was a priest moving round the altar, gathering hymn sheets. She crossed herself and walked hurriedly down the aisle. Hearing her footsteps he turned. She barely noticed his face as she knelt in front of him.

'Father' she whispered, 'please, please could yer 'elp me?'

'What is it my child?'

'Could yer read this to me? Oi can't read.' She handed him the pamphlet. He looked down at the sheet and frowned.

'It is not good reading.' He said. 'Why do you wish to know what this rubbish says?'

'Oi think it is talking about my daughter.' She broke down and sobbed uncontrollably. The priest, taken aback but with great compassion took the paper from her.

'Come my child and sit here', he said leading her to an empty pew. He produced a pair of reading glasses from inside his cassock and proceeded to read.

'The Lamentation of REBECCA DOWNING'
Condemned to be burnt at Heavitree, near Exeter on
Monday July 29th, 1782. for poisoning her Master,
RICHARD JARVIS.

by Elizabeth Brice

Good People all, pray, pity me,
And list to my sad fate
From birth the Child of Misery
in tears I now bewail.

Rebecca Downing is my name;
of sensual parents born,
Who n'ere in Holy Wedlock bound
left me a Babe forlorn.

No tender Parent's fondling kiss
e're turned my soul to love,
No due Instruction taught my feet
in virtue's path to move.

In gloomy ignorance I lived
scarce glimps'd Religious light.
What wonder, when temptation came
that I forsook the right?

Averse to labour's drudgery,
I sighed for Slothful Ease
And with a Master's murder thought
To purchase quick release.

The mortal poisen with his Food
I mix'd without delay
And now to satisfy his Blood
My life for his must pay

When to the fatal stake I come
And Dissipate in flame
Let all be warned by my sad doom
To shun my sin and shame.

May I thus expiate my Crime
And whilst I undergo
The Fiery trial here on Earth
Escape the Flame Below

(Exon: Printed by J Brice. Goldsmith's Street.)

43

CHAPTER VII

Elizabeth stared as if stunned in silence at the floor. The priest at last broke the silence.

'Some mercy will be shown.' he said. 'She will be strangled before she is burnt'. Elizabeth was jolted out of her misery. She had to find the way to Liverdole.

'Oi 'ave to give the executioner money to make sure he does.' she choked. 'Oi 'ave to get to Heavitree.' She ran out of the church stumbling over her feet. She headed for the East Gate. Exhausted she crept into a small alley and sunk down to the ground. Sleep came almost immediately.

Waking the next morning by the sound of many voices, she ran out into the main street, and as she ran she noticed groups of people of all ages, including children and babes in arms, starting to take the same road out of Exeter to Ringwell and Heavytree and she knew by instinct that she should follow. They were all heading for the Liverydole crossroads, the place of execution for all those condemned to death at the Exeter Assizes. As the crowd, with her in their midst got closer she could hear the sound of hammering. It was the temporary platform and gallows being raised for the forthcoming execution. Some of the crowd were talking amongst themselves, as if they were going to a village fair, but she knew that they were on their way to Rebecca's execution. Many would have been given the day off work especially. Others were waiting to follow the sledge Rebecca would be chained to and dragged along on, Still others were hurrying to get a better view. Elizabeth suddenly felt sick. She had to get there before in order to speak with the executioner. Finally she saw ahead of her the platform except it was not a hanging gallows as normal. For a burning you did not need a gallows! Already the stake was in place on the raised platform and faggots had been placed all round it. This was to enable the crowd to have a better view of the accused and her death. She had heard that in some cases the guilty would be hung on the gallows, then taken down and the body burnt, but here the guilty, in this case her daughter, would be tied to the stake, strangled by a rope from behind by the executioner, and then burnt. She could only pray that the executioner would not be too drunk to be able to put Rebecca quickly out of her misery before the faggots were lit.

As she approached the crossroads she noticed a small man in a frock coat and hat waiting by the side of the scaffold. She noticed him prod the stake and walk round the area of faggots. He looked quite unassuming, as though he was out for a stroll. Crowds were beginning to gather round and about, but there was no sign of the ghastly procession. She hurried forwards, and as she did so was approached by two burly officers of the law.

'Keep back' one of them said.

'Please sir Oi 'ave ter speak with the executioner.' They were used to seeing family of the condemned wanting to talk to the executioner so they called over to the small man,''ere Bill, u're wanted.'

'Bill' stepped down from the scaffold and walked towards Elizabeth. As he came nearer she noticed his pock-marked face and missing teeth. His coat was quite new but was stained and smelt of beer. 'Oh God,' she thought, 'Please let him be sober.' She clutched her purse between her hands. He leered as he walked towards her.

'Well, what 'ave we 'ere?'

'Please sir, it's moi daughter Rebecca.' She gasped, unable to finish her sentence for the sobs that came rushing out.

'Oh, its u're girl is it, come to pay me 'ave you? 'Ow much then to put the witch out of 'er misery 'efore the flames get 'er?' She emptied the contents of her purse into his hands.

'It's all Oi've left.' He slowly counted the money, now only about six shillings.

'Well, it moight be enough, but there again it moight not!' and with that he turned on his heals, and looking over his shoulder shouted,

'we'll 'ave to give the crowd their fun with this witch though won't we!'

In the back-ground she could hear the sound of crowds shouting and jeering. She watched as two small boys climbed a tree nearby to get a better view. Falling back from the scaffold she turned and saw in the distance what could only be the dreadful procession coming up to the crossroads, and she ran as fast as her legs would carry her in the opposite direction. Knowing she was deserting her first-born child again in her time of need. Knowing she did not have the courage to watch the awful spectacle. Remembering the pathetic figure of her daughter crumpled in the dark depths of the castle prison. Would she ever be able to live with herself again? Would she ever be able to understand why this terrible injustice had taken place?

PART 2

REBECCA'S STORY

CHAPTER I

Her first memory, why was the lady asking her? What was she doing here in this terrible prison asking strange questions? She didn't have memories, at least not the sort this lady would want to know. And why did she have a piece of paper and why was she writing down everything Rebecca wondered, because, truth to say, she had said nothing!

The screams, yes were they her first memory? Not her screams though. They were coming from an upstairs window. First there had been the pleading, and then the screams and finally the dreadful moans, like an animal in pain. She had crawled deeper into the straw next to the old horse to hide the sound of them. She had tried to block her ears and listen to the noise of the horse eating his feed. But still they had permeated her consciousness.

However truthfully those sounds were not her first memories. Rebecca plucked at her rags with bloody hands. She was manacled and shackled to an iron ring in the ground. Her leg irons chafed her legs when she tried to move, and as she crouched down in the dirt and greasy filth of the prison floor she closed her eyes trying to conjure up what this lady wanted. A room with a cot was what she now remembered; at least a straw mattress above ground, on a wooden framed platform of sorts above the one main room shared with another, Sarah, Joan's daughter, but never-the-less the cottage clean and scrubbed, and the smell of food, ah yes food!! Her nostrils started to respond to the memories. Soup, that was what she remembered. A pot above the open fire in the grate. It was her job as soon as she was old enough to stir the soup in the pot. She had many chores, but this was an easy one because she knew at the end of the day she would be given some of its contents, whatever they were, with bread. Large chunks for a small mouth, her mouth started to water as she remembered the taste and smell. They even had pasties. Sometimes if Joan was away for a few days attending a birth in the next village, these were made before she left and taken by the girls down to the common oven in the village to be cooked for their lunch. This was used by the villagers if they did not have enough kindling to make their own fires, or, as in her 'mother's' case, when she was away and did not want the girls to make a fire, and the two little girls, with strict instructions not to light one or 'play with fire' would take their pasties, left by her 'mother', to the village oven to bake. The use of this oven had to be paid for, 1 penny for a pastie, 2 pennies for a dish of meat which other villagers sometimes brought down. What she wouldn't give for a small morsel now. She was close to starving having only received a mug of stale water and a small piece of mouldy bread during the last forty-eight hours. Since the dreadful journey from East Portlemouth, to Blackawton, then to Totnes, overnight in their filthy goal, then onto Exeter she had hardly had anything to eat, merely stale bread and water. Again the lady, Mistress Brice her jailer had called her, asked her about her childhood, and Rebecca closed her eyes once more.

Her first memory of her mother was of a woman, a large, gruffy, bossy but kindly woman. This was Joan Hutchings, the midwife and occasional parish nurse for the village of East Portlemouth. She was to learn later that Joan was paid by the Parish to look after her, and was not her mother as she had originally thought. Her mother had deserted her at birth. This had been evident when she was told that her future lay as a servant to Richard Jarvis, to whom she was to be bound over as an orphan apprentice from the age of eight till she was twenty-one, unpaid and grateful for any small mercy! However her first few years were relatively happy. Joan treated her in much the same manner as she did her own daughter. Both girls were expected to do their share of the daily household chores, and were cuffed equally if they didn't. But the cottage was clean and they were fed and given clean clothes and a warm hearth to sit by, together with a certain warmth and comfort from their carer. Behind the one roomed cottage, very similar to that of most of the village, was a small plot or garden, and here were planted the vegetables and herbs that made up their staple diet and medicines, together with bread brought from the baker, or made with corn that had been gathered at gleaning time after the harvest, and cooked in the bread oven besides the open fireplace in the living room. A few chickens produced eggs which were greatly savoured and eaten with great reverence once a week, and a pig was kept in a small sty at the back of the little plot, ready to be slaughtered and made into bacon and salted meat for the winter. She remembered Sunday dinner, made from scraps of mutton or very occasionally, beef, flavoured with swedes, cabbages, carrots, shallots, leeks and wonderful suet dumplings. In the winter there would be bacon, eaten with chunks of bread and milk, and potatoes and turnips, lots of them, and sometimes fish, pilchards particularly, when the fishing boats came in and her ,' mother' went down to the beach to meet the boats and purchase their supper if there was enough money left in her purse by the end of the week. It had been a time of hardship but she never remembered feeling the hunger she felt now, or indeed had felt when with Richard Jarvis. And of course although the chores were hard and monotonous, she was never as tired or as cold or as unloved as she was up at the farm.

Could she read or write Mrs Brice suddenly asked her. Rebecca looked up, struggling to come back from her revelries to the present. No, of course not, the likes of her never went to school. There were few children in the village who did go to school, East Portlemouth did not have a Dame School, or any school, so the few, those with richer parents went by cart to Kingsbridge, but Rebecca was not one of them. Like Elizabeth, her mother, she did not even go to Sunday school because of no 'Sunday- best'. Joan attempted to teach her own daughter Sarah what little she knew, just basic reading, but Sarah did not go to school either. The two little girls would watch enviously as those few whose parents were well to do, left to attend Kingsbridge School. They would then be sent to do their chores. Or if Joan was away attending to a birth, they would be left to their own devices, to steal away down to the beaches to collect pretty coloured pebbles and try to catch the minnows in the rock pools. As long as they returned before dark and the chores were done, Joan would not be cross, and as long as they had finished their chores, collecting water from the well, weeding the vegetable garden, feeding the chickens and the pig, washing out their smocks once a month and hanging them out to dry if the weather allowed. Also cleaning the small living room and clearing and washing the few earthenware cups, saucers and basins, the wooden plates, the iron kettle and the main iron crock, all of which were used at every meal because there was only one cup and basin and one spoon each. Sometimes they were taken along with her to collect kindling and fagots from the local woods to use as fuel for the fire, and sometimes they would collect wool that had caught on the brambles in the countryside for Joan to spin on her spinning wheel into basic clothes for the winter. During harvest season they would also be taken along to help with the harvest. She remembered those times as fun and exciting, watching the horses pull the wagons laden with hay and straw, and the stooking of the hay for the winter. It was hard work gleaning, pulling the wild oats out from the fields of barley, and picking up the gleanings, the grain that had been left behind on the ground during harvesting, and it was during one of those expeditions, she must have been about four years old, that she first remembered seeing her future master Richard Jarvis. He was already an old man then, and sometimes had his grand-daughter Mary in tow. The little girl shrunk away from him, though he would always hang on to her hand and drag her with him. But enough of that, the lady wanted her earliest memories, her happy ones didn't she?

Market day, oh those days were fun! Once a month Joan would gather up her vegetables and eggs, and together with the girls take them on the cart to Kingsbridge together with others from the village ready to sell their wares at the town market. More often than not however it was a long walk with their goods bundled between them, or on a shared pack horse, but generally in company, with other children running along as well. Once they even went by boat up the estuary to Kingsbridge. Alighting at the peer Rebecca remembered other boats tied up alongside, being loaded with yarn spun locally by women in their cottages, for the serge makers in Exeter. The market took place along the quay. Stall holders had already set up their stalls, but Joan had spread out a cloth and laid hers down on the floor. There was a hustle and bustle of people, shouting their wares, haggling the price of goods they were purchasing, children running everywhere, grabbing pieces of sugar beet or the odd apple to eat off unsuspecting stall holders' barrows. Then the long walk home, tired but happy particularly if Joan had managed to sell all her goods. One time she remembered seeing an old man, the one she had seen in East Portlemouth wandering around usually drunk, come up to the place where Joan was setting up her goods.

'So this is moi grand-daughter's bastard is it then?' he had said.

Rebecca did not know what a bastard was, though sometimes the village children had called her that when she was at play on the beach. She knew it was a rude thing to be called, so she asked her 'mother' there and then. At first Joan had told her not to mind, but then the sorry story of her birth had come out. Rebecca barely understood the stigma, but what she did understand horribly was that her 'mother' was not her 'mother'. She remembered feelings of horror when she realised that the dirty old man was her grand-father. She remembered asking Joan where her real mother was and had been told she had been deserted by her. But as children do she put all this behind her, after all she loved her 'mother' so what did it matter.

Mrs Brice coughed loudly. 'Answer me girl' she said

Rebecca had not heard the question? She looked up.

'How was your master? Did he treat you badly?'

CHAPTER II

She was eight years old. Not very big for her age, with stocky legs, a ruddy complexion and a mop of straw coloured hair. She was strong though. She could lift a bundle of faggots. She knew how to tend chickens and pigs, and do her household chores. She even knew how to make a pastie. Joan had shown both the girls. One morning she had been told to put on her best smock and petticoat, at least the ones that was least torn, and after breakfast she and Joan, leaving Sarah behind, had headed up the lane to the main part of the village. From there they turned right past the church along the lane to Rickham, the next door hamlet.

'Where we going' she had asked.

'To see yer new Master'. She had been told.

'Who' she had asked.

'Yer're of an age to be apprenticed now as a servant, and Mr Richard Jarvis has agreed to have yer and be yer new Master.' Rebecca knew that other children of the poor were apprenticed and sometimes disappeared to go to other villages to work. She also knew that some left the area completely and were never seen again. Rumours abounded that these children had died whilst apprenticed, but none had ever come back. She knew that Mrs Crispin up at Rickham Farm took apprentices and wished that she had been chosen to go there. She had seen girls come home on the odd occasion who were apprenticed to Mrs Crispin and they had spoken well of her as a mistress. But Mr Jarvis, Mr. Richard Jarvis, he was an old bad-tempered widow, a slovenly unkind man. You only had to look at his grand-daughter cowering beside him when she had seen them in the village to realise what sort of a man he was. All the children of the village avoided him, and never went up Mill Bay Lane from Mill Bay to his farm 'The

Cot' if they could help it. The farm, or rather small-holding was down the lane from Rickham. It was also tenanted from The Duchess of Cleveland, but it's land was mostly along the cliffs and fields off Mill Bay Lane, the dark and overgrown path that led down to Mill Bay. Very occasionally, as a dare, one or two of the boys had run up the lane and had met Mr Jarvis coming down herding his few head of cattle. They had hidden in the undergrowth rather than cross him. His reputation as a mean and unfriendly man was well known.

Rebecca had felt a shudder of horror go through her as they mounted the steps to his front-door. At one time the farm house had been quite grand, at least by Rebecca's standards, now it was very run down. The path leading to the front door from the iron garden gate was barely visible through the weeds and brambles. It was a square stone house with glazed windows sitting in the cleft of a valley leading down to the beach on the estuary, with steep slopes either side and undulating stony land, a hard place to make a living. The windows were dark and unwashed, streaked with the dirt of many years. The door was raised up with two stone steps, not a lapse door, divided across the middle into two sections like that of Joan's cottage and most of the one roomed cottages of the poor, (the upper half kept open to admit light, the lower half shut generally to keep in young children and keep out animals and fowl,) but a solid wooden door with a porch surrounding it and a massive granite lintel, however it was peeling and unwelcoming. The house itself had been built in the lee of the hills to give it protection and shelter from the weather and the roof was of slate, not straw, though as Rebecca looked up she noticed many of them missing. There were two old barns either side of the farm yard with a well in the middle. An old dog, a sheepdog,

56

chained to a post in front of a wooden kennel, was sleeping in the mud, but as they approached he had woken up and started to bark. Rebecca loved animals and had spoken gently to him, and he had quietened down. Lagging behind Joan she had felt her tug her hand, dragging her towards the door. There was a rusty knocker in the shape of a hand clasped and facing inwards, and Joan rapped it twice. They had waited for what had seemed an age, when finally the door was opened. Peering from the gloom inside was Mary, Richard Jarvis's grand-daughter. With head bowed she mumbled a greeting. Joan had asked for Mr Jarvis and had been told he would shortly be there,

'but please to come in'.

They followed the girl in. Rebecca had seen her on occasions in the village, but never really taken much notice. She was never out to play with the other village children. She was quite tall and fair- haired with a pale complexion, and about twelve years old, wearing a grey linen apron over a similar coloured smock. She had wooden clogs on her feet, no better really than Rebecca's, but she did have stockings. She led them in through the entrance hall to the parlour. Rebecca had never seen such opulence before. Even though everything was dark and dingy she was impressed with the sheer size and amount of furniture. There was a long wooden table with a number of high backed chairs and even an arm chair. In the corner was a large wooden cupboard or 'buffette', about six feet high with wooden doors. It was here she later found out, that the best china and glass was kept. There was a fire-place with a mantelpiece, and on the mantlepiece were two brass candlesticks. Over it hung a painting. It seemed to be some sort of portrait, at least it was of a woman, quite a young one at that, looking down across the room. The grate was an open one with a copper kettle on a small tripod standing at one side. The whole thing was overwhelming.

'My grandfather will be with you shortly.' Mary had said as she left the room as the old man appeared.

Richard Jarvis had been a reasonably successful tenant farmer, the younger brother of Jonathon Jarvis and part of a large Devon yeoman family. He had been married but had been widowed many years before. Mary, his grand-daughter had come to live with him after his only daughter and her husband had both died in a cholera epidemic, when she had been four years old. He had become a bitter old man over the years, leaving the farm to moulder, barely making enough to pay his rent and feed himself and Mary, let alone another mouth. He had not wanted an apprentice, but realised the extra money would be a benefit, he would be paid a premium by the parish for taking an apprentice, and another pair of hands were now needed as he was unable to do as much in the fields as he used to. The horse and few cattle still needed tending, the fields needed clearing of stones and weeding, the turnips needed picking, and Mary was now taking the place of the farmer's wife, albeit begrudgingly. So he had agreed to take on a pauper apprentice. He had hoped for a boy, that would have been better and more useful, but he had been landed with a girl, and a simple one at that.

Out of the gloom a figure had shuffled through the door of the parlour towards Joan and Rebecca. Mary had backed against the wall as had Rebecca.

'So this is the girl is it?' he had growled. Joan had pushed Rebecca in front of her.

'She's a good 'ard-working girl, though a bit simple.' Joan had replied.

This was the first time Rebecca had heard herself being called simple, and was not sure of the word's meaning. She knew sometimes the other children had laughed at her when she did not understand their games, and sometimes Joan had shouted at her when she had forgotten to do one of her tasks, and sometimes she escaped into a dream world all of her own, where she didn't hear anyone or anything, but was that what the word simple meant?

Richard Jarvis had moved forwards, leaning on a walking stick, whilst his grand-daughter shrank from him as he passed, until he was standing in front of the cowering form of Rebecca. The smell of stale food and tobacco came with him like a shroud. He raised his hand and pinched Rebecca's arm hard.

'Ain't made of much, she better be 'ard-working, else she's no use to me!' Joan backed away,

She'll do what yer want sir, never yer mind, and Oi must be going.' With that she had turned and fled through the open door, down the hall and steps and out of the yard, leaving Rebecca alone in the darkness.

****

'Come on child' repeated the lady, 'I haven't got all day.'

Rebecca looked up and suddenly tears began to stream down her cheeks making channels in the dirt and blood on her face as she was jerked back into the present. That had been the last time she had really been happy. The next seven years had been too awful for words. Where should she begin? Yes he had beaten her, often and sometimes without mercy. Yes, she had been permanently hungry, but hers had not been the worst suffering, what about Mary?

'What work did you have to do child?' The woman's voice softened as she spoke.

From that first day it had started, the drudgery and

constant labouring. In many cases these pauper girl apprentices were allowed to sleep in the same bedroom as the girl children of the family, however Rebecca did not. On the day of her arrival, holding her pathetic bundle containing her bible, given to her by Mr John Jarvis on the occasion of her christening, virtually the only thing she had ever been given though she could not read, plus a clean overall, a pair of darned stockings and her favourite possession, a small cracked clay model of a horse with a small dog at it's feet, given to her by a passing peddler when she had helped to take a thorn out of his dog's paw, she had been shown to a small lean-to off the back kitchen, really no better than a stable. It contained a straw pallet, stool and bucket. No form of heating had been visible, although the small window at the side did have a shutter, which was open, letting in a slim shaft of light. Mary, for it was she that had taken Rebecca outside to the shed, had stood looking at her in silence, until finally she had said 'Not much, but at least yer' outside!'

A strange remark, but one Rebecca was to remember in the future. That evening she had been summoned to the kitchen, beyond the parlour, by Mary, where she had found the old man sitting at the kitchen table. 'Tomorrow yer'll learn yer chores girl.' He had growled. 'Sit down and eat now.'

Rebecca glanced round her and moved towards a large wooden rough hewn table with benches on either side and a large ladder-backed chair at the head. On one side of the room was a huge chimney place with an open fire over which were a number of pots and kettles hanging from hooks. On either side of the chimney breast, inside the fireplace were two small bread ovens and two shelves set into the brickwork, one contained a small clay pot. Although Rebecca did not know this was where the household salt, a valuable commodity, was kept in order to keep it dry. On the opposite wall was a large wooden dresser with a few tin plates and bowls haphazardly laid along the shelves Mary was at the fireplace, ladling soup from a cast iron pot into three bowls. Into two of the bowls she added a potato from another pot, and into the third she heaped four or five. On the table was a wooden platter with a half-cut loaf of bread, two tin cups and a large tin beaker and three tin spoons. There was a jug of water plus a large pewter jug of cider. Richard Jarvis reached across for the cider and filled his beaker to the brim, then reached for the bread and began to cut two thin slices and then one thick one. 'Come on girl, hurry up, what are you doing!'

Mary turned, head hung down, and carried the large bowl over to the old man. Rebecca noticed that she shrunk away as she laid the bowl down in front of him. He didn't look up but took up his bread and spoon. Rebecca also noticed, as Mary placed her bowl in front of her, that there were small pieces of meat in the soup as well as vegetables and potatoes. She couldn't believe her eyes, a veritable feast! Maybe life wasn't going to be so bad after all. Dinner was eaten in silence, only broken by the old man's slurping and grunting. He refilled his beaker until the jug was empty. At one stage Mary went to get up from the table.

'Sit down Mary.' he muttered. She slipped back into her seat. He turned to look at Rebecca who sat silently looking into her empty bowl. How she would have loved some more, but she missed Joan's homely cooking, even though the meal was much more substantial than she had ever had before.

'Well girl, I hope yer be strong enough for the work. Yer don't look it. Now help Mary clear and clean up, then to bed. Oi want yer up early tomorrow. Oi hope yer've more suitable clothes with yer, if not Mary will give yer some.' With that he left the room. Mary got up from the table and started to clear. Rebecca got up too and quietly asked what she could do to help.

'Are those the only clothes you have got? asked Mary.

'Yes, replied Rebecca.

'You can't work in the fields in those, I will fetch you some proper work clothes.' She disappeared from the room up the back stairs which led off the side wall of the kitchen. Rebecca followed her up the stairs and along a dark corridor, and walked behind her into her small bedroom. There was a small truckle bed in the corner with a quilt laid over it and a table and chair by the window. There was a wooden cross above the bed with the figure of Jesus hanging from it. Rebecca noticed a wash-stand with jug and wash bowl in pretty flowered porcelain in the other corner. Mary opened a leather trunk at the end of her bed. She pulled out a heavy smock and a pair of wooden clogs.

'These will be a bit big but they will have to do'. She handed them to Rebecca. As she walked across the wooden floor creaked. The two girls left the room and went back down again. There was no sign of the old man. Mary handed Rebecca a lit candle on a cracked saucer.

'Go to bed now, and don't heed any strange noises.' she said.

CHAPTER III

Rebecca slept a troubled sleep occasionally waking to the noise of the old yard dog barking. At one time she thought she heard a high pitched scream, but put it down to an owl. The next morning, before sunrise, she was woken by a heavy banging at her room door.

Old Jarvis appeared at the door, 'Get up girl, we've work to do and yer've to earn yer keep!' She struggled out of bed, rubbing sleep from her eyes. Pulling on the smock, her only stockings and the clogs she opened the door and walked towards the house. Breakfast consisted of a mug of liquid where the barley had been boiled and then removed for use later on at lunch, and a hunk of bread. Mary was already in the kitchen sweeping the floor. She had dark rings under her eyes and was very pale. Rebecca greeted her but she barely acknowledged the greeting, and continued with her sweeping, head bowed.

'Drink this up now.' The old man pulled on an old overcoat, 'Come we 'ave to feed the horse and cattle and chickens. Oi'l only show yer the once!'

Rebecca followed him out to the stable, across the muddy yard, past the dog who was by now barking at the end of his chain. Jarvis threw a bone to him which he grabbed at and slunk back into his kennel. The horse was in his stall, tethered to a ring by his manger.

''ere girl,' the old man pushed her past into another part of the barn where there was hay and straw piled up in one corner. He grabbed a large armful of the hay and took it through and placed it in the hay rack above the horse's head. Then he walked back to the same place. In the corner was a large wooden container with a lid on it. He took up a wooden bucket and lifted the lid. He then scooped out enough grain to fill the bucket half full and went back to the horse's stall. He emptied

63

the contents of the bucket into the manger in front of the hungry animal who all the while had been snorting and eying Rebecca as if she was something very strange. On receiving his food the horse immediately put his head down and started to eat.

'This'll be yer job every morning before yer've yer breakfast. Now follow me.' He took the bucket and walked back and refilled it from the grain bin. In the next stall were three cows, who now also received hay. He left the barn with another bucket full of grain and she hastened along in the dark behind him, trying to keep up with the stooped figure. Behind the stable they past by another round barn, open on all sides with what looked like a turning wheel mounted on a brick stand in the middle. In the corner were piles of apples. No wonder he drank cider, she thought, having seen these cider presses before on some of her visits with Joan. As they walked on round to the back of the old house the sun was beginning to rise above the hills. A broken down hen coop loomed through the dawn. A few mangy chickens were appearing looking for food. The old man shuffled towards them and threw the contents of the bucket onto the muddy ground in front of the coop. Those birds that were already out started to devour the grain, whilst more, clucking furiously, came pouring out of the coop. These appeared to be the only livestock on the farm. She had expected a few pigs as there was also a sty, but this was empty, or so it appeared, but through the gloom she caught sight of Mary, carrying a bucket of slops which she poured into a trough in the sty, and as she did one large pig appeared from inside the sty.

'Yer'll feed the pig too' Jarvis had said.

And so began her apprenticeship with Richard Jarvis. Each day, with no respite, she would be up before the dawn, and without any nourishment in her complaining belly, she would do the rounds of feeding the livestock, including the old dog, who mainly got scraps which she collected each morning together with the slops for the pig. After a meagre meal of a mug of barley water and a hunk of bread she would start the rest of her chores. Milking the cows was a chore she took to, relishing the warmth of their breath and bodies as she slowly thawed out, then driving them out to pasture, and back again in the evening. In summer she would weed the corn, set the potatoes, gather the apples, tend to the horse, and help the old man harness up when she was too small to handle the plough, then when she had grown take over the ploughing, then in the evenings it was her duty to help Mary with the household tasks, washing the floors, cleaning the cooking pots, washing the sheets, collecting firewood. She was rarely in bed before late evening, generally an eighteen hour day. Winter was the hardest as in all weathers she was out in the fields, hoeing the turnips and pulling them from the frozen ground, struggling through the deep mud to drive the cattle, breaking the water in the troughs, with cold wet freezing hands, now covered in chilblains. Oh those chilblains! Her hands and feet were never warm! Tending to the animals was one of the only joys. She would talk to them, and feel that they understood her. Her world was very silent, Jarvis never spoke unless he wanted something done or to chastise her, Mary barely spoke a word to any-one. She had become more and more silent and pale as time went on. If one of the animals was sick it was Rebecca who would stay up all night to tend them, administering the remedies that she had been shown by either Jarvis or her grandmother. Occasionally Jarvis would go to the cupboard in the kitchen and take out a jar of arsenic, used for the old horse if he was sick, and place a small pinch into his feed. It did seem to work.

Rebecca realised the woman was still in her cell. She looked up and Mrs Bryce watched silently as tears began to roll down Rebecca's soiled cheeks.

'That's when the beatings started was it child?' 'Oh no, she thought to herself, they started right at the beginning, but that's when they got worse.' Up till then Jarvis had contented himself with just cuffing her around the ear, slapping her around the face, or knocking her to the floor, generally accompanied by verbal abuse if she happened to be late in the morning or got a chore wrong. But this particular evening was when it all really started. She guessed she was about thirteen years old, there was no such thing as birthday's so it was hard to reckon, but she had grown about six inches and was way to big for her clothes. In fact she was now much taller than Mary, who had hardly grown at all. Mary's cast off clothes barely fitted her any more. It had been very cold and was early in the spring, before the primroses appeared on the banks of the tracks. It was evening, she was late she knew, but collecting the cows had been hard as she had lost her clogs in the heavy mud and as she had tried to find them the cattle had wandered off down the lane. She had managed to collect them but in fear, after having put them in the barn and fed them, hurried back to the house, knowing she would be in for a cuffing at the least, and probably very little to eat. Punishment of withheld food was used regularly. However she was not prepared for the dreadful night that was to follow. As she hurried round the back to the kitchen she caught sight of Mary re-filling her grandfather's mug. She knew instinctively he had been drinking the potent 'scrumpy' the dregs of the cider barrels, for some hours and she would be well advised to eat her meal in silence and slip quietly away. This was not possible. As she entered she heard him growl,

66

'Is that 'er? Oi'l 'ave her hide!' Mary looked at her with pity in her eyes.

'Get to yer room girl' he snarled at Mary. Rebecca wanted to run away but was frozen to the ground. He lurched towards her and grabbed her by her hair and dragged her over to the table.

'Yer idle good for nothing, 'cos of yer Oi've lost most of the fowl!' Rebecca looked over to where Mary had been but she was gone. Occasionally she had asked Mary to feed the chickens in the morning whilst she was doing the pig if she was running short of time and Mary had obliged, albeit begrudgingly, and this day had been one of them! 'The fox had 'em last night, yer didn't shut them up did yer|?'

Oh mercy, had she forgotten to put them back in their coop, she couldn't remember. She had been so tired last night she had barely had the strength to eat her supper, and had gone straight to her bed after. She noticed on the table the mangled remains of one of the hens, he grabbed it and thrust it into her face, covering her in feathers and blood. Hurling abuse at her he flung it on the ground, still holding her by her hair, which felt as though it was coming out by the roots. Then he started to unbuckle his leather belt. The beating she received was so awful. It hurt so badly and she willed it to stop. The pain didn't leave a lot of space in her mind for any other thoughts. Afterwards misery, rejection and feelings of unworthiness flooded into her mind. The effect of this dreadful change of dynamic was to make life such that, because punishment like this could happen at any time, no day was a safe day, a good day, until it was over. She resented not owning her own life.

From then on the days and nights blurred into one long space, filled with fear and hunger and the beatings continued, with Jarvis using his belt more and more and

67

finding more and more excuses to do so. She took refuge with the animals, often sleeping in the barn at night with them after her meagre supper. Sometimes she would start in her bed but then the strange animal noises would echo down from the house, and try as she might she could not block them from her ears, so she would move out to the barn where she couldn't hear them.

'What happened on the day girl?' The lady's voice broke through once again. Rebecca started. She had coiled even further into herself, trying to escape the awful feelings that welled up inside her.

'Oi dunno! All of 'em 'as asked me an Oi can't remember.'

She noticed that the lady had written a great deal down. Why it should be of any interest Rebecca didn't know, but the last question brought back horrible memories, memories of betrayal and terrible fear.

'Come girl you must be able to remember something! Mr. Jarvis is dead, poisoned, God rest his soul, and his granddaughter has given a statement, one that has persuaded the judges of your guilt, and all you can say is that you did nothing wrong and you don't remember. Tell me anything, I need some information, and it may help you live!'

Rebecca looked up to the ceiling of her dark cell. What did the lady mean? She had done nothing wrong, it had all been a mistake, of course she was going to be set free, and then she would be able to go back and work for Mary. Without the dreadful cruel old man things would be so much better.

The horse, she remembered he had been sick with colic the night before. The old man had been angry and blamed her, saying she had over-fed him. He had slapped her across her head and then he had dragged her to the kitchen and reached for a jar from the top shelf of the old dresser. 'Take this girl, this is arsenic. Yer've seen me give it to the 'orse 'efore, give 'im half a spoon-full in 'is feed tonight. No more mind, too much 'll kill him, and Oi'l hold yer responsible for that!'

She had taken the jar and a spoon out with her to the stable. Making up the bucket she had added a carefully measured out the amount as he had said, and mixed it in with the feed. Adding an apple she had kept in her pocket for later, in case the horse had refused his feed because of the taste, she gave it to him. He did not seem at all put off and tucked into the bucket eagerly. She had crept back to the kitchen clutching the jar and spoon. Mary was alone when she got back. Rebecca gave her the jar and spoon and watched as she drew a chair alongside the dresser in order to reach and put the jar back. She placed the spoon in the basin and rinsed it out. She glanced round at Rebecca as she did so.

'Have to be careful,' she said, ' a pinch can kill a man!'

That night, after supper, during which Old Jarvis had drunk two jugs of cider dry, she had escaped as fast as she could. On her way back she had detoured round to the stables to see how the old horse was. He was munching away at his hay happily, so she went to her bed, curled up and prayed for a good day tomorrow, where the old horse was well, and she would make no mistakes that would warrant a beating. They had become more severe and were now a common occurrence. How she hated him and every night wished him dead!

She woke up with a start. It was still very dark and she could hear screams, then sobs then moans coming from the upstairs windows. She clambered out of bed, putting her hands over her ears. These dreadful sounds had also been coming now most nights. How she dreaded them. Wrapping her shift round her she ran across the yard to the stable and barn. Sinking down into the straw bedding in the old horse's stable, the noises now no longer, she crawled in amongst it, taking care to be away from his droppings. The noise of his breathing had slowly comforted her and she had drifted off into sleep.

The next morning came and she had crawled from her hay bed back to her room. Putting on her working clothes as fast as she could she had run to the barn to feed the cattle, horse and then the pigs and hens. She had returned to the kitchen in the hope of some breakfast. As she had entered the room she had seen Mary pouring out some barley water from the jug into her grandfather's mug, then her own. She had passed Rebecca a hunk of bread, but no barley water, making the excuse that there was not enough and her grandfather was hungry. Rebecca had eaten the bread and started to move out of the kitchen towards the barn to gather the cattle to herd them out to the fields. As she had crossed the yard she had heard a shout. Mary had run out into the yard shouting and clutching her stomach.

'Hurry quick and call the doctor, grandfather is sick as I am too.' Rebecca had run quickly out of the yard and up to the nearest farm, which happened to be Rickham, and shouted for help. The old farm hand, hearing her shout, had called for his mistress who had run down to the 'Cot'. Rebecca followed frightened and worried. She thought she had better get on with her chores, or risk another beating later so she headed for the barn. That evening when she returned to the house having fed and bedded everything, she noticed Mary standing outside the door. She looked even paler than usual and Rebecca had asked after the old man. 'The doctor is with 'im now, 'e might die!'

Rebecca was shocked.

All night the doctor came and went. Mary had recovered from her aches and was very agitated. There was no meal that night and Rebecca went to bed hungry. The next morning she woke to hear the sound of a horse trotting across the yard. Thinking it was the doctor again she ran across to the house. But it was not the doctor, it was the constable from East Portlemouth. He was accompanied by the doctor who had been at the old man's bed-side most of the night until he had died in the early hours, and who was still within the house, which had happened, Rebecca had been told subsequently, shortly before dawn.

'Come 'ere girl' the constable had called to her from the scullery door. Shaking with fear she had crossed the yard and entered the scullery and then the kitchen. Mary was seated at the table weeping and red-eyed. Clutching her skirts and ringing them through her hands she had looked up as Rebecca had come into the room and she had exclaimed,

'It was her, I saw her do it! She put the poison in the jug! She put some in mine as well which is why I took sick too, but she refused to have any herself.'

Rebecca had been bewildered.

'What do you say to that girl?' the constable had asked her. She had tried to remember what had happened the previous morning. She remembered the jug and she remembered Mary pouring its contents into the old man's mug, but whether she had had any she could not remember.

'I gave her some and she refused to drink it.' said Mary, looking accusingly at Rebecca.

'She poisoned him I know she did.'

Rebecca stood routed to the spot.

The doctor spoke to the constable. He would have recognised unnatural death having nursed the victim till he died.

'Call the churchwarden, his brother, tell him he has been allegedly poisoned by his apprentice, Rebecca Downing. We need to have a witness statement from his grand-daughter.'

'Yer coming with me girl,' the constable said to Rebecca.

'But what about the old 'orse and cows, they need milking, and pigs and hens?' she had asked?

'Never mind them, yer 've more serious things to think about. Go fetch yer belongings and we'll get the cart and take you to Totnes where yer'll be held until we find out what he died of.'

Rebecca did not understand really what had taken place She had understood that her master was dead, and for that she was not sorry, in fact she had suddenly felt an overwhelming sense of freedom. Life without him would be tolerable with just her and Mary. She had no problem with that. She had gone to her room and taken up her things, all of them because when she came back she hoped she would be able to move into the house as there would be a spare room now!

CHAPTER IV

On returning to the kitchen she noticed that John Jarvis, the old man Jarvis' brother and church warden for East Portlemouth was sitting talking earnestly to Mary at the kitchen table. She overheard him say

'Are you sure girl, this is a very serious accusation?' Mary looked over to Rebecca, then away again. In a whisper she said

'I'm sure.'

'Very well' he replied. He had then called Rebecca into the kitchen,

'Sit down girl, I want to ask you a few questions'. Rebecca had obediently sat down opposite him.

'Rebecca, how do you know which jar contains the arsenic for the horse. Can you read?' Ashamed she had replied

'no sir, me master always gave me the jar'. John Jarvis remained seated for a while in silence, then he left the room. Calling the constable who was waiting outside, he said

'I have a horse and cart, you may use that to take Rebecca to Totnes to the magistrate there whilst preliminary investigations can go on.' I will ride on first and tell them you are coming so they can prepare the jail. Now I need to speak with Rebecca.'

'Come here girl.' He beckoned her over. Nodding to the constable he gestured for him and Mary to leave the room. Rebecca crept over and sat down at the table. She had never been afraid of John Jarvis as she had been of his brother. She had no idea of his involvement in her up-bringing, having been the person responsible for putting her into Jane Hutchin's care when she was abandoned by her mother.

'Rebecca, are you aware of what you are accused of doing?' he asked her. 'No sir.' She looked down at her clasped hands.

' Do you know how your master has died?'

'Yes sir.'

'Rebecca, did you prepare the barley water for breakfast yesterday?'

'I don't remember sir'. She truly didn't. Living a day at a time was the way she managed to get through her life. Sometimes the days blurred into one, especially if she had had a beating and was trying to keep out of the way.

'Mary sais it was you who prepared it that day. She sais you poured it out for her grandfather and herself but took none yourself, is this true?' 'Oi don't remember sir.'

'Mary said you must have put arsenic from the jar above the range into the jug and tried to poison them both. She said her grandfather had shown you where it was in order to dose the horse. Did you?'

'Yes sir, Oi dosed the horse with the medicine me master gave me. Why would Oi put some into the barley water?'

'I don't know Rebecca. Why would you? Did you like your master?' 'No I hated him!' This was out before she had a chance to think.

'Why did you hate him?' She looked down again at her hands,

'He beat me bad', she whispered.

John Jarvis was a fare man, not embittered like his brother had been and he had heard the rumours of the way his brother treated the young apprentice girl. He was a successful man in the village and Mary was his grand-niece. He was amazed to see how contained she had appeared to be after the death of her grandfather, and how her accusations against Rebecca were uttered with such conviction. It still puzzled him how she had taken a drink from the same jug as her grandfather and survived, just being, as she said, a bit sick. Richard Jarvis had drunk a whole mug, according to her statement, that was why he had died and she had survived.

'Rebecca, did you refuse to drink any of the barley water?'

'Oi don't remember sir.' John Jarvis was well aware of the seriousness of the accusation against the girl.

'Can you read girl?' he had asked. She had hung her head ashamed,

'No sir'.

'Then do you know which jar holds the arsenic you use for the horse?' 'Only when moi master gave it me sir.' She had replied.

John Jarvis was troubled, crimes of petty treason, in other words the murder of a husband or master, carried the sentence of death by strangulation and burning. The best the convicted could hope for was deportation. But he knew that these transportations to the Americas were now ending. What terrible punishment would be meted out to this girl. However blood was thicker than water and the possibility of any involvement of Mary could not be allowed. It would reflect on the entire family, so any doubts he had were quickly removed from his mind.

Calling for the constable he had turned to Rebecca.

'Come child.' With that he moved towards the door of the kitchen and down through the hall to the front door and the yard. Rebecca had sat on the chair unable to move, almost as if she was unaware of what would now happen. She remembered quite clearly seeing Mary peer into the kitchen then quickly disappeared. The constable had come into the room. He had moved towards her and in his hands he had held cuffs and ankle chains. He had bent down as she sat and placed the cuffs on her wrists. All the time she remembered not really taking anything in, that is until he had pulled her out of the chair.

'Come on girl, the judge is waiting for you!'

'Where are you taking me?' Why am I chained?' She had collapsed on the floor at this stage, and he had dragged her outside to the waiting cart.

She had started to scream for Mary. Where was she, the one person who could vouch for her? What was happening, why was she being treated like this, she had done no wrong? In the yard was a drovers cart and driver with an old horse in the shafts. Mounted on another horse alongside was Mr John Jarvis. As she was dragged up into the cart she glimpsed Mary across the yard.

'Mary, whose going ter milk the cows and feed the animals? Promise me you will whilst Oi'm gone. Oi'll be back soon'. Mary, white as a sheet had fled into the house.

The cart had rattled along the lane from Rickham to East Portlemouth. Although Rebecca did not realise, word had already got back to the village and most of the villagers were out along the track. As it passed with its sad and frightened passenger crouched down in one corner, the villagers stared, first in silence,

'Witch, witch,' reverberated around the lanes, 'kill the witch!'

One had hit her on her back and the constable, who was sitting alongside her, had tried to protect her. Other missiles, rotten vegetables, and excrement were also thrown. Finally John Jarvis had cantered up. Shouting at the many who were now alongside the track to stop, he had ridden alongside the cart.

Are you hurt Rebecca?' he had asked.

''Oi'm alright' the terrified girl had replied. 'Where' we going?'

'To Totnes' he had replied. 'You will be safe there.'

The cart slowly trundled it's way north to Totnes with its miserable cargo. The carter never turned round to look at the child crouching in the corner. The constable rode alongside her occasionally telling her to stop snivelling. Finally arriving after dark it mounted the narrow steep main street of Totnes till it came to the small jail house half-way up on the right, close to the church. There were few people about even outside the taverns which were at either end of the street. The tired horse came to a halt outside and the carter climbed out and the constable dismounted and tied his horse to a hitching ring on the prison wall. John Jarvis had left them at Blackawton, saying he would continue on to Totnes the next morning, but that he should get back to take care of his niece Mary. As he had ridden away Rebecca had called out.

Please sir, don't leave me.' But he had ridden on without turning. Bumped and bruised she was half lifted, half dragged out of the cart. The jailer appeared after having been summoned by the carter.

'Well, what 'ave we e'ere?'

'A murderer of 'er master' announced the constable.

Rebecca was pulled through the small door into a dark room where the jailer obviously lived. It contained a fireplace, a chair and table and in the corner a trundle bed with an old mattress. The jailer peered through the darkness,

'why she's only a girl, 'ow long is she to be here?'

'Only the one night.' remarked the constable, 'then on to Exeter ter'wait 'er trial.'

'Follow me,' said the jailer, jangling a heavy bunch of keys. The constable, dragging Rebecca behind him by her cuffs, followed him through a door, down a dank corridor, till he reached the end which was blocked by another door, this time with bars covering the small aperture in the door. The jailer reached for one of the keys and unlocked the large lock and swung to door open. The room was windowless with a damp earthen floor making it smell of damp and old urine! In the darkness Rebecca could make out a bucket, and nearby, half-way up the wall, an iron ring. Shrinking back she whimpered,

'Oi don't want to go in there, please sir. It's so dark'.

'Get in girl', said the constable, and moving across to the ring, he manacled Rebecca's hands to it.

'Oh God, please sir, don't leave me 'ere', she begged. He ignored her and the jailer, who had left the cell, for that was who it was, came back in with an old tin jug of water, and a hank of stale bread.

'ere girl' he said, and taking the keys from the constable he released one of her hands, and handed her the jug. 'Drink!'

Rebecca gratefully took the jug, spilling it in her haste, and drank thirstily. She had been given no food or water since early that morning when she had left Rickham. Taking the jug back he handed her the hunk of bread. Realising how hungry she was she grabbed it and started to eat. The constable looked at the jailer with surprise.

'What yer do that for? he asked.

'She looks hungry, and she be about the same age as moi daughter'. was the only explanation the jailer would give.

The constable shrugged his shoulders and went out of the cell with the jailer following him. The door swung behind them, clanked into place and Rebecca heard the sound of the key being turned in the lock.

Alone in the darkness she dropped the bread. She tried to reach down to retrieve it but found that still being shackeled by the one hand she was unable to do so. Neither could she sit, but had to remain half standing. Loud sobs broke from her. Trying to make sense of what had happened that day she paused and tried to wipe her eyes with the one available hand. She had done nothing wrong, so why was she being treated this way. A dog barked in the distance, and somebody shouted out to tell it to cease. Suddenly she heard the key turning in the lock, and as the door opened she saw the jailer come into the cell. He moved towards he and she shrunk away into the wall. As he raised his hand she screamed. 'Hush girl, Oi'm only trying to help.'

And with that he took his keys and released her shackled hand. As she sunk to the floor he said,

'Now try and get some sleep'. With that he walked out of the cell and closed and locked the door. She was once more plunged into terrifying darkness.

Sleep came mercifully, even though the floor was damp and hard. Dreams of strange happenings had filled them. Mary was crying and pointing a finger at her grandfather, and then at Rebecca. And all the time the cows were mooing and crowding round her as if to protect her. She had woken with a start as the key in the door clanked and it opened. The jailer, rubbing sleep from his eyes, came in carrying a bowl of a sort of porridge and a wooden spoon and some more water. Rebecca, who was still struggling to get up, thanked him.

Eat up girl you'm to be ready for 7 o'clock, and tis now 6 o'clock.' He started to leave the cell,

Did you kill 'im?' he had asked as he turned.

'No sir' she had answered.

'Why should they think Oi did. Leastways Oi don't think Oi did.'

She had tried to remember, and then it had all come flooding back. The accusations, the dreadful journey,

79

and the fear of having possibly unknowingly done something terribly wrong.'

'Eat girl' he had repeated.

'Yer'l need all the strength yer've got to survive the jail in Exeter!'

After the meagre meal she had tried to gather her thoughts, but not many minutes later she heard the key turn again in the lock of her prison door. As she struggled to her feet again she looked up to see the constable standing over her with the shackles in his hands.

'Get up girl' he said ' we 'ave to be moving on.'

'Where to sir?' she had asked. He had looked down at her with a strange expression on his face.

' Be yer simple girl? Yer 'ave a date with the magistrates!'

Rebecca stood very still as he placed the manacles on her hands, and this time more round her ankles. Her clothes were by now filthy. She had barely managed to reach the bucket, and there was no water to wash in. Her hair was hanging in straggles and although she had not been that concerned about her appearance before, the mention of the word magistrate put the fear of God into her mind. She had to look good for them. She felt, in some strange way, that this was important. She tried to run dirty fingers through her hair and straighten her smock. It did not make much difference, but somehow she felt less unworthy. She had, in the back of her mind, the words of her nearly forgotten 'mother' Joan Hutchins, that it always helped to have clean clothes on for the law. She couldn't do that, but at least she should make an effort. 'Cleanliness is next to Godliness' It had to help, and she needed help to understand what was happening, and to cope with what was going to happen! Shambling along behind the constable, because that was all she could do with the leg irons fixed round her ankles, she blinked as she came out into the cold light of day. It was barely dawn, and thankfully there was no-body around apart from the horse and cart and carter that had carried her to Totnes the previous night. The constable climbed into the cart instead of on his horse as before. Rebecca did not realise, but parish money had run out and could not afford to pay for a horse for the constable any longer.

'Where am oi to go sir?' She had asked, worried that she would be in the way.

''Ere girl,' he had held out a hand.

Surprised at his kindness she had taken his hand as he had pulled her into the cart. Landing in a heap on the floor at his feet, she had managed to pull herself up into a sitting position. The carter had clicked and the horse, acknowledging his shake of the reins had started to move off with his passengers. Rebecca had turned around to glimpse the jailer; he was standing outside the jail with a disturbed look on his face.

'Good luck girl,' were the last words she had heard as the cart slowly wound it's way back down the hill to the bottom of the town, over the bridge and back up towards the main road to Exeter.

CHAPTER V

The bumpy cart tracks had started to even out and become more or less roads. The jolting and swaying had lessened somewhat. The horse had stumbled less and his pace had quickened. The carter had not sworn as much under his breath and the sun had slowly risen in the east. Rebecca, clutching her smock in her manacled hands had tried to remember. She was cold and hungry and dirty and frightened. At this time she should have been feeding the cattle and horse. Who would do that now? Who would make sure the old dog had water, and the chickens, what about them? The constable was talking softly to the carter and she couldn't hear what they were saying. She had gazed over the edge of the cart, watching the cart wheel go round, lost in thought. She had never travelled farther than Totnes before, so the trip should have been exciting, but of course it wasn't. Fearfully she searched for signs of life in the hedgerows and banks. Perhaps there would be a friendly face, or at least someone who could explain what was happening, and indeed where she was going. After what seemed like an eternity, but in fact was a few hours, the cart approached Countess Wear. Their only brief stops had been for the men to leap off and pee in the hedges. Rebecca would have liked to do the same but was too embarrassed to ask. By now the rest of the world was awake. The cart did not attract much attention, word had not reached Exeter yet about the murder. It would take a few days at least for the information to reach the pamphleteers. Then they would have a field day, but in the meantime the cart passed along the roads unnoticed. Even the constable's presence did not arouse suspicion, probably because constables did not wear special uniforms yet and so could be mistaken for ordinary passengers. The small girl huddled in the corner went completely unnoticed.

She noticed the smells first, much the same as her mother would those weeks later. Then she gazed, amazed, at the cathedral high up in the centre of the city, towering over it and overlooking its walls and river. As they approached the city walls and gates the rabble from outside, in their rags, were already gathering to go in. Young children, dressed in tatters, helped push small carts laden with what appeared to be produce for the markets. Mules laden with bales of cloth, woven in the small outlying villages, and driven by large men, passed them by. The smell of the butchers shambles strengthened as they headed towards the city. Ahead, up against the city walls was the meat market where carcases of whole sheep and cattle were being carried through the streets and alleys, the sight of which brought tears to her eyes. She once again remembered her charges. She had, of course, seen dead animals before, but not in such quantity, nor skinned. Dogs followed the smells, yapping at each other, fighting for the blood that dripped from the dead newly slaughtered beasts. After an uphill climb, with the poor horse struggling to keep his feet on the slippery cobbles, they reached the East city gate, abutted by great walls on either side with a wide street beyond, itself bordered on either side by tall gabled buildings. Passing through it the carter suddenly reined in the horse. A small boy leapt forward and grabbed the reins from his hands.

'The jail be the other end of the town'. he remarked,

' I got some business to attend to first.'

No yer don't ' snapped the constable 'first we go to the other end where the goal is, in the castle .'

The carter shrugged his shoulders, then grabbed the

83

reins from the boy and climbed back aboard the cart. Hitting the old horse on his rump with a stick they moved off up the street. On either side were many tall buildings with shops below, the like of which Rebecca had never seen before. Half timbered dwelling houses were also interspersed on either side. There were also houses with windows for the wealthy. Carriages passed along the way too, their passengers hidden from the outside by curtains at the windows, their horse or horses in smart harnesses, their drivers in smart liveries. Rebecca stared open-mouthed, her hunger and discomfort forgotten, completely amazed by what she saw. So many people now, ladies in coats and hats with feathers, tip-toeing along the muddy pavements, trying not to get their shoes dirty. On the corners boys shouting with pamphlets and newspapers in bundles by their sides, not as yet telling her story! They passed a large building set back from the street; it was one of the new hospitals, springing up around the country, to become known as the Royal Devon and Exeter Hospital, founded in 1741.

The city goal was still in the medieval South Gate of the city. Slowly the cart moved through to meet with the High Street and turned left into it. Ahead, bordered on both sides by tall gabled houses, and with twin turrets either side above the gate was the old caste, and goal. Rebecca did not know this was what it was, but felt a sense of gloom and despair as they travelled along the street towards it. Even the carter seemed to sense the mood as his head sunk down deep into his shoulders. The constable glowered at him.

'Get a move on, we ain't got all day!' he said.

At last they came to a halt outside a large studded door in the left turret. Rebecca looked up at the towering building ahead of her. Barred windows looked down from the centre portal above the gate, and to either side in the turrets. She sensed rather than saw watching eyes, and shuddered. The constable leapt down and pulled at a chain hanging by the door. A bell could be heard, ringing inside. For a while nothing happened. By now there was a small crowd gathered round the cart. Rebecca shrunk down as far as she could, hiding her legs and hands, trying not to show her manacles and chains. Voices started asking questions.

'What she done then? Are they goin ter hang 'er?'

Small boys started to try to climb up into the cart. The carter pushed them off.

'She ain't been tried yet, so never yer mind!' A man's voice was heard above the rest.

'Oh ay, well we'll know soon enough. The pamphlets 'll tell us!'

The constable pulled the chain again, and the door opened almost immediately. Rebecca, still crouched in the cart, could not see who had opened it, but heard a voice growling from within. She could not hear with clarity the conversation, but after about three to four minutes the constable returned, red in the face and holding his nose.

'By God it stinks, and the turnkey is drunk! Oi couldn't get any sense out of 'im.' The carter said nothing.

'Come girl, get down now.'

The crowd had moved away, though there were still a couple of wide-eyed urchins hanging around staring at Rebecca. She struggled to her feet, and lurched towards the back of the cart. Half stepping, half falling, she found herself in a crumpled heap at the feet of the constable. Pulling her up by the chain between her manacles, he dragged her towards the door. She would never forget the terrible stench that greeted her, nor the terrifying noise from behind the door. Though it was dark, and she could see nothing she could hear mumbling, wailing, moaning, screaming, pleading, angry hysterical voices all mingled together. The apparition that came through the gloom into the light was foul, filthy, loud-mouthed and drunk. She had seen the like when old Richard Jarvis had been in his cups. Dribble and drool ran down his stained front, urine seeped out of his breeches, and he was swearing loudly under his breath.

She tried to hide behind the constable, but he was eager to pass her over and have done with it and get back to better places. He handed over some paper work. The turnkey laughed

'Oi can't read!' he leered at Rebecca.

'Oi'l get the jailer', and with that he lurched back into the gloom.

****

The voice of the lady broke through her memories.

'Well girl, are you sorry for what you did?'

'Oi did nothing,' she had whispered.

And as she had been dragged down through the dark endless passageways and stairs, she had said the same to the jailer. He had not listened, pulling her by her shackles along and down till at last she was jerked to a halt, somewhere, she thought, in the depths of a hell she had imagined as a child when threatened with it by Joan! In front was a wooden door, greasy and stained, with a small grill in a tiny opening and a large bolt with an even larger padlock on the outside. The jailer had produced from his belt a large ring, onto which were fastened dozens of keys. Selecting one he had unlocked the padlock and opened the door. Inside there was no light, at least not enough to discern how big the space was, all she remembered was the nauseas smell of stinking damp earth, stale urine and the decomposing bodies of rats, a smell she was familiar with because it had been her duty to empty the rat traps in the barns on the farm. Thrusting her forward the jailer picked up from the floor an old iron ring attached by a rusting chain to a metal plate in the wall. Linked to this ring was a pair of leg-irons. Forcing her onto her knees he placed the irons round her ankles and padlocked them shut. Too dazed to realise what had happened she remained in that position long after he had left the cell, slamming the door closed and locking her in. Slowly she began to look round the gloomy dark space she was now confined in. The room was about 10ft by 10ft, with no light save what came through a small window in the door which was itself covered by bars. As her eyes became accustomed to the gloom she could make out what appeared to be a rusting tin cup with dirty water in the corner. She managed to crawl across as far as her shackles would allow her to and reached the cup. Draining the filthy stale water produced some relief to her parched throat.

She crawled back to her corner and started to weep. Soon her long drawn out sobs echoed round the walls, and she wept till she finally could weep no longer.

CHAPTER VI

That morning the jailer had arrived early.[2]

'It's yer special day terday girl, yer day in dock,.

What was 'dock'? She had never heard the word before. She had seen the stocks in Kingsbridge on occasions.

'What's dock sir'? she had asked.

'Yer'll see' was his only answer.

Dragging her by her wrist shackles, still with her leg-irons on, she was propelled up from her cell to the gate of the prison. Here was waiting the drovers cart and two constables this time. The cart contained two other passengers besides the driver. A man and a woman both sitting and wretchedly staring at their feet. She sat down next to the woman, who shuffled away from her as far as she could. The cart moved off, with a crowd gathering to follow, and headed back up towards the centre of the town till it finally halted outside the Magistrate's court. Then it was taken round to the alleyway alongside and the three prisoners were taken off. Two constables , taking up each of their shackles, lead them down some stairs under the main building and placed them in a large cell, locking the door behind them.

Rebecca looked up at her co-prisoners, both were now hunched in separate corners.

'Yer the girl who killed 'er master ain't yer?' one of them, the man, had looked up and spoke to her.

'Oi didn't, at least if Oi did Oi don't remember.' She had replied.

The sound of keys turning in the lock was followed by the cell door opening and the jailer signalled to the woman to get up. As she left and the cell door was

---

slammed and locked again, the man had turned to her and had raised his head.

'Don' expect no mercy 'ere, oi'm sure to swing! But yer'll burn yer poor wretch'.

In shock she burst into tears again and shrunk down into the corner shaking and trembling. She did not notice when the jailer returned without the woman , though she had heard the noises coming from the courtroom above, the shouting of the crowd, and the scream. The man had looked up at that and remarked that the woman had been branded for blasphemy. At that time the sentence would have been carried out in the courtroom immediately after the judge has passed sentence. Branding on the forehead was done in front of the jury and the crowd in the gallery so they could see justice being carried out.

She remained huddled in the corner for what seemed an age, during which time the man had been taken out and returned, this time shaking and weeping himself. He had been thrown into the corner, after which the jailer had pulled her to her feet,

'Yer turn now girl'. With that she had been propelled up the stairs. As she mounted them the noise from the crowd increased until at last she reached the entrance to the court. Cringing she was led by her manacles up the stairs into the dock.

There was a jury, made up of local farmers, tradesman, publicans and yeoman. Rebecca did not realise it was such but here were twelve good men and true! She stood in the dock on a small stool because she was too small to see over otherwise, manacled and handcuffed. On her right, sitting at a desk on the lower level was a bespectacled man with a quill and ink and paper. He was already writing, scribbling like fury. Rebecca could not read, of course, but she watched fascinated as he dipped the quill, with its long feather, repeatedly into the small pot, and drew it out dripping with ink. Opposite her were two benches enclosed by a railing, and behind this railing sat twelve men, and she could count up to twelve having been taught by Joan. They were a mixed assortment, some in wigs and frock coats, some with greasy hair down to their shoulders in smocks and breeches. They were all looking at her fixedly. She tried to shrink below the parapet of the dock to avoid their stares. To her left were two distinct areas behind tables, one contained two bewigged gentlemen, smart and upright, clutching large amounts of paper. Above, at the back of the court was the public gallery. The noise of those crammed into the rows, and it was overflowing, was terrifying to the small girl cringing in the dock. She sunk as far down as her shackles would allow her. Suddenly the clerk of the court, sitting below the judges bench stood up and demanded the court to be silent and 'upstanding for the judge, His worship Sir Richard Park and accompanying magistrates, Thomas Taylor, Buck Fortesque Esq., John Laroche, James Pitman, and John Burridge.'

The public gallery fell silent as did the rest of the court and the door opened behind the bench. Firstly all but the judge processed onto the platform, dressed in their frock coats, and breeches and high boots, all gentlemen of the city, exuding wealth and pomposity, not a kind face amongst them. Of course this was not surprising, her crime was a particularly heinous one, that of petty treason. It was an offence considered worse by the authorities than the more common one of murder, since it amounted to the killing of someone to whom the accused had been subject to.

The clerk had approached her.

'Rebecca Downing you stand here accused of the crime of petty treason in that on the 24th day of May 1784 you did feloniously and traitorously poison your master Richard Jarvis. How do you plead, guilty or not guilty?'

She stood mute, too frightened to speak.

'How do you plead girl, guilty or not guilty?' he asked her again.

'Guilty!' – it came out suddenly before she could stop herself. It seemed easier to accept Now perhaps she could go home.

There was a gasp from the crowd in the public gallery. She looked up and caught a glimpse of John Jarvis and Mary sitting on the front row. She raised her hand to waive, thinking they were there to take her home, but realised she could not because of the manacles round her wrists which were attached to the bench

She had noticed the lady who had visited her in the prison and written all those notes scribbling away furiously in the public gallery. Then the last thing she remembered was the judge placing a black cap on his head. Looking at her he repeated these words

'Rebecca Downing, you have been found guilty of the heinous crime of Petty Treason, and for this you are condemned to death. On Saturday next the 27th July in the year of our Lord 1784 you will be drawn on a hurdle to the place of execution, and then burnt with fire until you are dead.'

Her return to Exeter prison was recorded in the Western County Goal Book, under the heading 'Devon Summer Circuit 1782 22nd July. Pd.

'Rebecca Downing; For feloniously and traitorously poisoning and murdering Richard Jarvis her late Master as in the indictment 'Petty Treason. The said Rebecca Downing, following the Coroner's inquisition is to be drawn upon a Hurdle to the place of execution on Saturday 27th July instant and then burnt with fire until she be dead. Resp. till Monday and then let the execution be done.'

As can be seen there is no mention of her being strangled first!

CHAPTER VII

Bemused Rebecca looked around her dingy prison once more. Shackled again to the floor she sat on the cold wet ground shivering. She had barely remembered the journey back from her trial in the cart. She had dim recollections of the judge asking her to plead guilty or not guilty. She had been so frightened, and so unsure of what to say, but she remembered saying if they thought she was guilty then she must have been. She had not meant to hurt any-one, though to be truthful she was sure she had not put the poison into the mugs. When the judge had put a black cap on his head and she had been told to stand, after the jury returned, she had noticed a hush fall on the crowd in the room. She had heard the word 'guilty', she heard the word 'executed', and she had heard the word 'burnt'. She had heard 'three days hence'. She had heard the gasp come from the crowd when her sentence was read out. Within minutes there was an uproar in the courtroom. She had noticed the woman Elizabeth Brice stand up in the public gallery. She had a piece of paper in her hand and she had obviously been writing. Rebecca had watched as if in slow motion as the woman pocketed the piece of paper and left the gallery, running out as if she was followed by the devil. Within seconds Rebecca had been dragged out of the court, with her shackles clanking and with the noise of the crowd still ringing in her ears. Everything had become a blur as she was bundled out into the yard behind the court room and heaved up into the waiting cart. The journey back to her castle prison was noisy. The crowd had streamed out of the courtroom to meet the waiting throng outside.

Once in her cell with her ears still ringing from the crowd's shouting she was shackled once again to the iron rings. Exhausted she fell into a troubled sleep, on and off for the next day or so, only to wake when the jailer refilled her mug with filthy water or threw a maggot ridden crust at her. She awoke two days later to hear her cell door being opened. A woman huddled in an old serge cloak too big for her small frame, stumbled through the darkness towards her. The jailer muttered to the woman that he would be back shortly. The woman then whispered something to him, and next thing Rebecca's chains were being removed. He closed the cell door behind him and she heard the grating as the key turned in the lock. Rebecca looked up hopefully, desperate for food and water. She struggled to her feet though her legs would not hold her, and as she stumbled the woman rushed forwards and touched her shoulder. 'Who are yer?' She whispered to Rebecca something about her being her long lost child,

'Oi'm yer mother.' The woman was now sobbing,

'Oi don' have a mother.' Rebecca had replied.

'Oi don' have a father either, and Oi killed me master!' Where was the food she so badly needed, and where was the water? Who was this woman? What did she want? Realising there was no food Rebecca cringed away from her, struggling to break free as the woman took her hands in hers.

Rebecca sank to the floor once more, and she started rocking, back and forth whilst Elizabeth took her hands once again.

'What's going ter 'appen to me?' Rebecca asked,

'why am Oi 'ere?' she demanded again. The woman tried to put her arms around her. Rebecca recoiled again.

'Are they going to let me go tomorrer?' she had asked.

'Oi should so like to go 'ome'.

'Yes, yer going home tomorrow' the woman had

gently said, through sobs,

'Just close yer eyes all the way there and yer'll reach home.'

'Who'm Oi going to work for as me master is dead?' Rebecca had demanded. She could even take the beatings if she could go home. She could work for the mistress, her dead master's grand-daughter couldn't she. Mary would be needing more help now he was gone, and she was the only one that could cope with the horse. Rebecca looked up at the woman again,

'Go away'. she said,

'Oi don't know yer! Oi'm going home tomorrer any way so Oi 'll get food then.' The door to her cell opened and the jailer lurched towards her, keys in his hands. He knelt to shackle her back.

'Well witch, ' the warder growled,

'Time to put yer chains back on to make sure yer don't fly out the

window 'efore tomorrer and yer big day!'

He bent down and placed the fetters back. The woman turned as she reached the door, she looked at Rebecca, and through her tears, she muttered good bye. The door banged shut and again the lock grated as it imprisoned her once more.

Witch, What did 'e mean? She were no witch. She remembered hearing the same word being shouted by the crowds as she was brought back to the prison. And now the jailer was calling her a witch again. She remembered, with horror, the children in the village accusing her of being a witch's granddaughter when she had been very small. She would go running back to Joan and cling to her apron, frightened and confused. Joan would lay a hand on her head and tell her to take no notice. She wished Joan was with her now to comfort her. The door opened once again and this time the jailer held a large mug and a piece of bread. He handed her the mug. It did not contain water, but she recognised the smell. It was the same beer that her master used to drink every night. 'Ere girl, drink this. It'l help yer sleep and prepare for yer big day tomorrer! She took the mug. Occasionally she had managed to drink the dregs from the old man's mug so she knew the taste. It had always given her a warm feeling, so she drank to whole mug down now. By the end of it and after eating the bread she was feeling decidedly woozy, and for the first time warm. Sleep came once again, but less troubled this time.

In the Exeter Morning Herald, dated 10 August 1782 appeared this paragraph:

'On Monday se'nnight, Rebecca Downing, for poisoning her master, was, pursuant to her sentence, drawn on a sledge to Heavy tree, near Exeter, attended by an amazing concourse of people, where after being strangled, her body was burnt to ashes. While under sentence, and at the place of Execution, she appeared totally ignorant of her situation, and insensible to every kind of admonition, though she acknowledged her guilt.'

On that morning she had been roughly woken by the jailer, with what she had assumed was a mug of water, though not from her bucket. He thrust it towards her with a growl,

'Ere girl, drink this, yer mother has paid for it, and it'll help yer through the day.' She struggled to her feet as he unlocked her manacles. Taking the dirty stained mug she took a sip. The smell was recognisable, she had smelt it before on old Jarvis's breath.

'Whoi yer giving me this?' she asked him.

'Just drink it girl.' He replied. It was like fire water, a clear fire water, but with a strange taste. It was the first time she had ever tasted gin. By the time she had finished the mugful she was already feeling woozy!

She sank to her knees, holding her head. He came in again, this time grabbing her up from the floor. Pulling her, for by then she was feeling very sick, they mounted the stairs up to the ground level and through the entrance to the prison.

She heard before she saw the noise of the crowd. She saw in front of the gates an old horse, hitched to what appeared to be a large wattle panel which was lying on the ground. Before she knew what was happening she was thrown down on the panel and tied to it with rope, passed through her hands and round her neck. The rope was tightened so she could hardly breathe. She was vaguely aware of the horse moving forwards, dragging her on the sledge behind. All the time the crowd was shouting and jeering, and again calling her 'witch'! She felt something sting her side and realised that they were throwing stones at her as she went through the town gates. The dreadful journey took over forty minutes. The bumping and jolting was horrendous, until the awful procession, which is what it was by then as she had been followed all the way by an ever increasing crowd, came to a halt. Through her hazy thoughts came the realisation that they had stopped, and she was being lifted from the hurdle, and looking round she laughed through terror when she saw a small boy fall out of a tree nearby. A rough looking man came towards her and grabbed her and placed her on the raised platform and secured her to a stake sunk into the ground beneath the platform by an iron chain round her body. A cord was put round her neck and passed through the stake. Two cartloads of faggots (bundles of dried brushwood) were then piled around her as she tried to regain her conciousness, it was then she saw the woman who had visited her in hospital, standing on the edge of the crowd, staring in despair at her. She felt the executioner move behind her, then she was aware of flames, the heat started to come up from her legs.

She heard a scream and realised it was her own voice as the flames started to rise higher round her body, the pain was unbearable, then mercifully she felt the rope round her neck start to tighten.

Part 3

Mary's Story

CHAPTER I

She had not wished to go to the execution, in fact nothing on earth would have dragged her there, but her uncle, John Jarvis had insisted she went. 'To see justice done!' But was it justice? Her grandfather was dead! And good riddance! At last she was able to sleep at night! No more the noise of the heavy treads across the corridor, the terror and disgust building up inside her head. No more taking of the foul potions given to her by Rebecca's grandmother when her 'termes' were late. This had occurred twice when she was much smaller, later she learnt, from the grand-mother, to use a cloth soaked in vinegar! She had been sworn to secrecy by the grandmother and her grandfather, when she had given her the potion after being taken to see her one cold winter's afternoon.

She no longer lived in her grandfather's house, it had been rented out to another tenant farmer shortly after Richard Jarvis' death. The Duchess of Cleveland's Factor had made sure that there was no gap in the rental monies! The farm had to be farmed. The old horse had been sold together with the cattle to pay off her grandfather's debts. All his goods and chattels had been auctioned off as well. She was to receive the monies obtained from the auction, but as yet had not seen a penny. She was lodging with her uncle John Jarvis, and her aunt needed the money she was told, as part of her keep. So she had nothing! Now she had some inkling of what it was to be poor, and at the beck and call of some-one, but at least she didn't have to live with the fear of those dreadful nights. She had kept house for her grandfather ever since her parents had died and she had been sent to live with him. There had been one other paid hand before Rebecca, then her grandfather had become too old to farm the land

101

efficiently enough to have any spare for paid help. He had decided to take Rebecca in spite of the fact that he really needed a boy. Mary had hoped another girl in the house would make a difference, but it didn't. She tried not to remember the day the murder had happened. Once she had accused Rebecca there was no going back! Had her grandfather not died from the poisoning she knew she would have taken a knife to him one day.

Sometimes she would try to remember her parents. They had both died of cholera within a few months of each other. She had been ten years old. She remembered her mother well. She had been an only child and much loved. They had lived in a small village near Exeter, her father had had something to do with the wool trade, and her mother had kept a neat tidy house, with rooms upstairs and downstairs and a small garden out the back. There was never a shortage of food, and always much laughter and happiness. When the epidemic hit the deaths had been shocking and sudden. Her father had been the first, and her mother had nursed him till he died, only to die herself shortly after him. She had been brought to live with her grandfather after the death of her mother. She had not known him well. He had lost his wife many years before she was born and had lived alone since then. For a small girl of ten, lately orphaned, it was a terrible shock. Going to a remote farm house, with only an old man for company. A demanding old man who told her in no uncertain terms that she was now his housekeeper and should look after the house and his every need, just like his wife had done before!

CHAPTER II

Mary could read and write small amounts. She had been sent to Sunday School at the church in East Portlemouth, after she had moved in with her grandfather, to learn her chatechism from the Rector of the time, James Grantham. There was no school in the village, even a Dame School. She had learnt the catechisms by rote. Daughters of the house were needed to do the chores round the house. Mary was familiar with some of those having helped her mother before. If her mother had lived she would have imparted all her household skills and knowledge to her daughter. She had had to take on the full burden of a household whilst her mother lay ill and dying but missed out on later teachings that only a mother can impart... For Jarvis it meant an unpaid housekeeper. Certainly she had been kept busy and she had seen the appearance of Rebecca as a bonus.

She remembered thinking , as Rebecca entered the house for the first time that maybe now he would turn his attention to this other younger girl and leave her alone. She had just turned twelve when he had first come to her bedroom, drunk and filthy. Sitting on her bed as she tried to crawl further down beneath the covers. That is when it all started, and continued till the day he died. The only respite was when he had beaten Rebecca, for then for some reason he seemed satisfied to leave her alone, till that night he beat Rebecca so hard she thought he would kill her. That night he came to her room once again, this time like an animal. She had screamed but, from bitter experience she knew no-one would come to help her. She knew she hated him enough to kill him.

Coming to the trial with her uncle those few days before was an ordeal she never wanted to repeat.

103

Wearing her best clothes she had followed him to the Courts of Justice in Exeter. She had been warned by him to remember her story in detail. Well she had hadn't she! They had climbed the stairs to the public gallery and she was made to sit in the front row next to her uncle. Clasping her hands together she had looked over at Rebecca. Oh how dreadful she looked. In rags and chains, filthy dirty with a large cut down her tearstained face, her hair straggling down her back. She looked so starved and thin. Although it had not been good at her grandfather's at least Mary had managed to put food on the table regularly for the both of them. She had never intervened when he had taken his leather belt to Rebecca, and for this she suddenly felt remorse, but somehow at first it had helped hoping he might leave her alone when the beatings occurred.

However it had not been so, in fact his visits became more regular after the arrival of Rebecca. The hopes that a female apprentice would be used the same way as she had been had been in vain. Rebecca certainly go the beatings, but that did not seem to satisfy the old man completely. At first she had tried to fight him off, , but finally during the last few years she had given in, only pleading when he was so filthy and drunk that he had turned to violence. Hatred had come easily and with it the thought of ridding herself of him. Uncle John had all but accused her – but had fallen short, remarking that families had an obligation to protect themselves and their good name. The memory of what had happened on the day and night before he finally died came flooding back

About an hour later, after she had managed to get her grandfather to his bed, the doctor had arrived. She was sent from the bedroom, but she could still hear the old man wretching down in the kitchen. The doctor had come down stairs and asked her what they had had for breakfast. She gave him the jug with the remains of the liquid in it. He had smelt it, and dipped his finger into it.

'Who made this brew?' he had asked.

'The apprentice girl did sir'. She had replied.

'Where is your apprentice girl?

'She is out in the fields doing 'er chores sir.'

'Did she sup with you?' Mary had panicked at this moment.

'Yes sir, but she refused to drink anything. It was her that poisoned my grandfather'. She had exclaimed.

'He had looked at her strangely, 'poison you say, and where might that be?'

'On the shelf there' she said pointing up to the overmantle,

'e uses the arsenic in the jar to doctor the horse when 'e is sick. That was where Rebecca was when Oi called her to sup.' As she had uttered the words accusing Rebecca her uncle John Jarvis had ridden into the yard. He had heard in the village that his brother was very ill and had come over immediately. Dismounting he had come into the kitchen just as she had shouted out her accusation of Rebecca. She had blushed and looked away, unable to meet his eye as he had stared at her.

'That is a very strong accusation Mary', he had said, 'Are you quite sure?'

'Yes uncle, I am sure, look even I was sick after drinking, and she 'ad 'ad none and had refused to take even a sip.'

The doctor had returned to the old man's bedroom.

'Go sit with him girl, I have to take this jug to have it tested, arsenic you say? I will be back later' and with that he had ridden off leaving her with her uncle.

John Jarvis had been a kindly man, so different

from his brother. She had often wondered if he had known what dreadful things had gone on in this house.

'Please sir, I don't want to go and sit with him, I don't know what to do.' Mr Jarvis had looked at her, nodded and mounted the stairs.

She had continued on with her household chores as if nothing had happened. There had been no sign of Rebecca, probably not surprising after the terrible beating the old man had given her the night before. By mid afternoon she was still away. Her uncle was still up with her grandfather.

'I will stay till the doctor gets back', he had said. The late afternoon came and the old man was getting weaker, groaning and still being sick. She heard a horse clatter up the yard and watched as the doctor dismounted and then she had gone to the door to let him into the house. At the same time her uncle had come down the stairs.

'It's poison alright, and most likely arsenic.' The doctor had said to him. 'Is there anything we can do?' her uncle had asked the doctor. All night the doctor had remained. John Jarvis went home later on. Rebecca had come back in the evening and waited at the kitchen door. Mary had looked at her, and when she had asked if there was any supper, had told her no, her grandfather was still very ill and might die, and that she should go to bed. She remembered how Rebecca had given her a strange look, and then quickly slipped out the door, closing it behind her quietly.

Later on that night, or rather during the early hours of the morning she had heard the doctor leave her grandfather's room and go downstairs. She did not follow but lay there, shivering and frightened. As dawn rose she had dressed and gone downstairs. She heard Rebecca outside feeding the chickens and cows and geese, and the old dog bark as she had thrown him a bone. The doctor was sitting at the kitchen table.

'Your grand-father is dead.' Where is the apprentice girl?' he had asked. 'She's outside feeding the animals'.

At that moment her uncle had ridden in to the yard. He had come into the kitchen and told Mary to leave the room whilst he spoke with the doctor. A few minutes later he had called her back in.

'Sit down Mary'. She had sat down opposite him.' Are you aware how serious the accusation you have made against Rebecca is?'

'Yes uncle'.

'And are you sure that is how this dreadful deed was perpetrated?' She had swallowed hard.

'Yes uncle.'

'Very well, leave now and call for Rebecca to come to the kitchen. I wish to speak with her privately'. Mary had left the room as the doctor was leaving the house.

'I shall send for the undertaker' he had said, 'and for the constable, and a carter.'

'Why a carter sir?'

'To take the girl to Totnes and Exeter for her trial.' She had stood a while watching him mount his horse. About half an hour later the constable had arrived. She had watched from her window as Rebecca was lead from the house in manacles. Strange to say she felt no pity, just relief. Her uncle had also mounted up as the carter arrived. She had watched as they loaded Rebecca onto the cart, and it rattled out the yard, with the constable and her uncle riding either side.

'Your aunt will be along soon Mary to take you back to East Portlemouth to lodge with us till this is all over' he had said over his shoulder as they rode away from the farm.

'Thank God' she had breathed a sigh, she would

never have to live in this dreadful place ever again.

The trial had been awful, and as Rebecca stood in the dock memories of the day flooded in. Uncle John had told her she may have had to appear as a witness and be cross examined. as it was her accusation of Rebecca's guilt that had brought the trial in the first place. She was terrified. She had been made to wait outside when they had arrived at the magistrates court by her uncle whilst he had gone off to have a word with some important people he had told her. She knew he knew the judge and a number of the jury, so she had been greatly relieved when h had come back and told her she would not have to appear as Rebecca had confessed to the murder and would plead guilty.

'Can we go home then?' she had asked

'No Mary, we must stay and we will go up into the public gallery' he had replied. So there she had stayed, She was aware that Rebecca was in a complete daze, unaware of what was really going on around her, but even so she gasped as she heard Rebecca reply to the question,

'Guilty', as had the all those in the gallery. She had watched in horror as the judge had placed the black cap on his head, and she had heard the dreadful sentence being pronounced. Numbed and feeling feint she noticed her uncle look sideways at her,

'Come child we must go to our lodgings'

'Can we go home now sir?' she asked again.

'No Mary, we must stay to see the sentence carried out, we are family and it is expected.'

CHAPTER III

They had both stood back from the scaffold. She had watched in horror as Rebecca was dragged from the hurdle. The girl seemed to be insensible to what was going on around her, and laughed when she saw a small boy, who had climbed a tree to get a better view, fall out if it. She had watched, transfixed, as the girl was half lifted, half dragged to the scaffold. She had turned to her uncle, standing white faced, next to her, holding hard onto her hand. She had tried to turn away as the executioner had tied the chains round the girl at her waist, and then round the stake. She watched as he then passed a rope round the girl's neck and passed it through the hole in the stake, leaving it's ends hanging loose behind. She had tried to hide her eyes but her uncle had growled at her,

'You need to watch this young lady,'

Two other men then had dragged bunches of faggots onto the scaffold and placed them round the sagging body. Rebecca did not seem aware of what was going on at all, and had just shaken her head a couple of times, as if to clear her mind. The executioner then took his place behind her, and the mayor, or that is who she had thought it was, proceeded to read out the crime Rebecca was being executed for. Only then did Mary start to cry. Silently her shoulders shook. She prayed that all around her, for by now there was a large jeering crowd, would think it was because she had known the girl, not that guilt flooded her mind.

God knows she had wanted him dead so many times. She wiped her eyes and watched in horror as the men lit the faggots. The flames roared into life, and as they did she noticed the executioner move behind the body, which by then had let out the most dreadful screams, head up in the air and open mouthed, gasping for breath. Although she could not see what was happening she had been told by her uncle, in graffic detail, what would happen on that day, when he had taken her aside before the trial and asked her again and again if she had anything to tell him about the day the old man had died.

The flames had then taken hold and engulfed the small form so that it was no longer visible. The smell of burning flesh permeated the air. As the flames died down the crowd began to disperse, their afternoon's entertainment over. Eventually there was just a pile of ashes at the foot of the burnt out stake. Her uncle had turned to her once again.

'Come Mary, it is all over now for the best. Let us go home to forget this dreadful business. Let us remember family comes first!'

CONCLUSION

As seen in Elizabeth Bryce's article, Jarvis was a hard man, and was known to beat Rebecca. It is quite possible that he could have assaulted Mary as well. Could this explain Mary's accusation? There is very little information on Mary, only that the Jarvis's were a large influential family in the area. Any hint of scandal would have affected John Jarvis' standing in the village, and indeed in Kingsbridge. Thus his acquiescence in Mary's accusation of Rebecca can be understood.

Mary had been known to be a shy quiet child, not mixing with other children in the village. Withdrawn and sullen a lot of the time, shrinking away from her grandfather when in his presence. These symptoms now would be recognised as those of a child being regularly abused. It is possible that the arrival of Rebecca took away the beatings, but imagine the scenario, that of a single man living in close proximity to a young girl, albeit a family member, and wife who has been dead for a while. The farm was isolated, down a lane away from the village. Mary would not be seen from one week to another, and if she was it would have been in the company of her grandfather, a known violent and bad tempered man. Rebecca was too simple to have realised what had been going on. Maybe, just maybe Mary had been driven to the point of no return. She was 18 years old. She knew where the arsenic was kept, and could have read the name on the jar. She was the one who prepared the morning breakfast, the barley water for all three of them. She knew how much her grandfather drank, and she was clever enough to have understood that she too should be taken ill, in order to substantiate her innocence. She knew that Rebecca had taken another severe beating the evening before, and had shouted to the world her hatred of Jarvis. She also would have known of Rebecca's linking to her grandmother and the accusations of witching, which would have made the village generally against the girl. Could it be possible that, after years of systematic physical and sexual abuse she had finally had enough and decided to murder her grandfather? She had the motive and she had the time and she had an alternative suspect, a simple one who could not have understood the implications, to pass the blame to. We shall never know!

The tragedy is that if this had happened only a few years later Rebecca might have at best been deported, at worst hung. She would not have had to go through the dreadful sentence passed on her. For a pauper apprentice, particularly a female one, the odds were stacked against her from the very beginning of her short, sad life. So much for the 18th century being a period of Enlightenment. It was very selective and if you fell outside the selection life was as bad and as hard and unjust as it had ever been!

FOOTNOTES:

PART 1

Chapter 1
Page 1 In the deep lanes of rural South Devon the sledge and the pack horse were still in use There was hardly a pair of wheels in the county. Pack horses were the norm, laden with fish, wool and produce for the towns from the fishing villages dotted along the coast, or returning with cloth, coal and kitchen ware and with sometimes pieces of lace and leather shoes for the well to do,

Page 3. The hierarchy of the village was divided into three parts, the landlords, together with the tenant farmers and the clergy, the employees, house servants, farm labourers, men who crewed the fishing boats, and finally the 'undeserving' poor. Elizabeth's family were part of the third. Those that were on the parish poor lists, living on the charity of the others, a liability and an expense to the village in general.

Page 6. Clothes, breeches and smocks for the boys, smocks and petticoats for the girls, that had been made from home-spun material in the cottages of the better off who had spinning wheels, and then sewn by journeymen who travelled from village to village and house to house with their apprentices,

Page 8. Families tended to use other family members to crew the boats in order not to share the meagre income gleaned from fishing.

Page 9. Now in the eighteenth century these women and their knowledge had been marginalised, partially by the male encroachment into medicine and partially by the destructive attitude of the church and its woman-hating dogma. Still though, in small remote villages, women relied on other women who had knowledge of

113

herbs and their medicinal properties for the care of the sick and the poor, those who were with child, those who could not conceive and those who were desperate not to become pregnant, or if pregnant with an unwelcome addition to the family to feed, to rid themselves of the child. Now the standing of these women had declined rapidly in the big cities, and women herbalists were only allowed to practice if they could afford to buy a licence, which many couldn't. However in most country villages like East Portlemouth there could still be found a 'wise woman', an expert in the practice of medicine, birthing and birth control. These women, although unlicensed, were still expert in the art of healing and continued in their age-old traditions of preventative medicine, herbal remedies, and dietary healing. The poor were able to afford these remedies, even though they could not afford the new male physicians and doctors, and besides which there was a widespread distrust of doctors of every type, especially those who had infiltrated the birthing chambers.

Page 10. These remedies were a closely guarded secret within the women's sphere. The quantities an even more closely guarded secret because to get them wrong could cause serious illness, even death, and to be found prescribing them to prevent an unwanted birth was punishable by death. Wild herbs were still believed to be more effective than cultivated herbs for these medicines, particularly when needed for troubled women in the later stages of pregnancy, who had missed their 'termes'(menstruation) more than once!

Chapter 2
Page 16. In rural villages when a woman started in labour, it was the custom to send for the women neighbours to help in the delivery, partly to bear

witness to the child's birth, and partly to spread the knowledge of midwifery, because in an emergency any woman might be called to minister to the mother and baby. The miseries that some women had endured, and she had seen, when an unskilled midwife was all that was available, were too horrible to contemplate.

Page 17. In the 18ᵗʰ century, this 'period of enlightenment', approximately one in twenty five children died within24hrs of birth or were born dead, and the risk of the mother dying in childbirth was also high.

Page 18. A declaration made during or shortly after childbirth was considered applicable for use in court if witnesses were there to hear the mother's accusation. This was done so the mother could bring a paternity suit against the father.

Chapter 4

Page 27. Most of the production involved in sergemaking took place in the cottages of the workers. Independent weavers would buy the wool from the market, their wives would spin the thread, and the unfinished cloth would be sold on. Alternatively, the wealthy clothiers would finance and control all operations. Looms were often rented out by the Overseers of the Poor. It took approximately six spinners to keep a loom working. The whole town, like Halwell, and the countryside around would have been employed in spinning, weaving, fulling, dyeing, drying of serges, and finishing. The finished cloth was taken by pack horse to Totnes, and then on to Exeter to be used for army great coats, and men's jackets and breeks, but rough cloaks for the poor were made from the discarded pieces of cloth thrown out as unfit for making clothes for the wealthy. Some of the best quality serge was shipped to London to be made up into garments there too, but most was kept for local use.

Page 28. This wear, no longer in existence but an important land mark on the map, had been built in 1282 by Lady Isabella Fortibus, a countess of Devon, who had owned part of Topsham. Lady Fortibus had decided to build this barrier over the river Exe in order to raise the river levels to allow leats to power her mills. Originally ships had been able to pass this original wear but the Countess' successor Hugh de Courtney, of the powerful Courtney family of Exeter had closed this gap forcing trade to pass through Topsham docks which he owned. Henry Vlll had allowed the town of Exeter to remove this barrier as trade had been badly affected by it, but the river was never navigable again up to Exeter quay, and the subsequent road built by John Trew in 1563 in order to allow goods to reach the centre of Exeter again was the road that Elizabeth would travel along. However the area of the old wear still kept the name Countess Wear in memory of the original.

Chapter 5

Page 30. Like all those that worked in the prisons, from the governor himself downwards to the lowest turnkey, this man had paid a serious sum of money to secure his position in the prison and he needed to exploit his power as much as he could in order to earn back his investment. In Exeter goal things was particularly bad with the warder asking payment for water he brought in as there was no running water, the goal did not even have a chaplain or surgeon to administer to the prisoners. The gaoler charged fees for the prisoners for various services as well as water, and in addition he held a licence to sell beer to the prisoners. Of course that small comfort would not have affected Rebecca as she had no money!

Chapter 6

Page 46. England, with lively politics and a prominent role in continental war providing an insatiable market for news, and as a result of the development of the press in the late 17th century, the production of news pamphlets and journals was stimulated by the lapse of the Licensing Act. The lapse of this act, which had sustained a political and religious censorship and limited the number of printing presses, journalists and pamphleteers, now gave a free hand for publication of sensationalist news. This was read voraciously by the public, and one of the favourite forms was that of pamphlets with commentary on the lives of those about to undergo execution, generally sold both prior to and at the event. In 1715 a newspaper had been founded in Exeter by Joseph Bliss, who began printing 'The Protestant Mercury or The Exeter Post-Boy' at his house outside East Gate near to the London Inn. His venture came to an end by 1718 but his apprentice Andrew Brice made a more lasting market. Brice, the son of a shoemaker, who was educated at one of the academies of the period, broke his articles of apprenticeship with Bliss and founded 'The Exeter Post-Master in 1717, which was replaced in 1725 by 'Brice's Weekly Journal'. As well as being a prolific writer he was a poet and prologue play-writer. This journal was carried on by his son and his son's wife Elizabeth Brice. It was she in fact who was to gain a reputation for writing the histories of the condemned criminals to be sold to the crowds who gathered at their executions. This pamphlet that Elizabeth noticed being sold in the streets the day before and today was just such a thing. The noisy vending of trial and execution broadsheets was on a mounting tide during the 18th century. These were often produced alongside ballads written.

Page 51. The last women to be burnt alive without being garrotted first for petty treason, the crime of murder of either a husband or a master, the crime Rebecca had been found guilty of, was Catherine Hayes in 1726. However women continued to be burnt *post mortem* until 1790 when parliament abolished the burning of women for treason. In spite of this being the era of technological innovation which was affecting the design of everything from Bath chairs to water-pumps, the techniques for execution was so little touched that the process was still basically medieval.

PART 2

Chapter 2
Page 63. In 17th rural England it was the practice to apprentice pauper children, both girls and boys, to farmers. Sometimes the farmers did not have a choice, other times, and it was so in this case, the farmer received money from the parish for taking in a young child. This money was supposed to be for the cost of their keep, for clothes, food and instruction in a trade that would be useful for the apprentice in future life. In reality parish children could be bound apprentice at seven, work for their keep and often without any hope of learning a useful trade. Girls were bound until they were twenty-one unless they got married earlier. This apprenticeship system had been designed in the Middle Ages to provide vocational training as part of a regulated system of labour relations and was, at that time, dependant on the guilds for regulating. However in the eighteenth century the guilds were losing their power and the system no longer functioned efficiently. The openings now for parish children, particularly pauper children, were dead-end jobs, in which the master often took the child solely for the sake of the £2-

3 premium that the parish paid him so as to get the child off its books. There were many cases of illtreatment, and in some cases of death caused by starvation and beatings. The *Newgate Calendar* lists a number of cases. In most these children became mere drudges, a form of slave labour, without the parish taking any responsibility for their welfare, only to glad to have them no longer an economic burden. The farmers who took these children found them useful, cheap labour and undemanding about the farms.

Page 69. Pauper apprentices in the eighteenth century had no rights. Politically pauper apprenticeship was intended to be a form of social control, and parish officials acknowledged it as a reliable method of keeping down the poor rate. The rules of indenture were strident. The pauper child was to 'demean him or herself' towards the master and all his family, behaving' honestly, orderly, and obediently'. The work of a young female pauper apprentice on a farm was arduous, and the hours long. Days started at dawn till dusk and then there were the household chores. She would have to be up at dawn, feeding and attending the animals, pigs, calves, horses and poultry, leading the horse to plough, dropping potatoes, digging potatoes, (potatoes and turnips were the staple diet of the labouring poor) helping with the hay-making and harvesting, picking up stones from the fields before ploughing, pulling turnips, a winter job and one of the hardest as it involved pulling them from frozen ground in the freezing weather, even in snow. During a frost or in snowy weather it was not uncommon to see boys and girls of 9-10 years of age crying bitterly on account of the cold, their hands so blue and numbed they could scarcely grasp the turnips they were engaged in pulling. They would work all day and then return at night, take off their wet clothes to dry and often put them on in the morning again still wet. The female pauper apprentice would also have been responsible for helping as a maid-servant in the house, cleaning and washing on a daily basis. There was very little time off and punishments were considered the right of the master. Regular beatings were acceptable and in fact expected. There was no supervision of apprentices by the parish once they had been placed, and cruelty was common. Run-aways occurred, but for girls the only alternative was prostitution.

Chapter 3
Page 84. Medical expertise did not play a significant role in English investigations until the early nineteenth century, and forensic pathology until a century after that. Much earlier the testimony of medical practitioners was heard in court, and ordinary witnesses would search human remains for signs of unnatural death using common sense and traditional wisdom. Discoloration of some of the organs, together with the symptoms suffered by the afflicted were recognisable as arsenic poisoning though.

Chapter 4
Page 89. Eighteenth century pauper children, especially girl children, were not educated. It was felt that as their station in life would never be better than basic servitude they did not need or indeed warrant time spent on teaching them to read or write.

Page 95. Parish constables were elected once a year by the vestry meeting in each parish. It was an unpopular job and unpaid. They wore no uniform but had truncheons as a badge of office.

Page 99. Hospitals provided valuable medical treatment for the common people, but they also served the interests of their masters! Trainee physicians and surgeons got the bodies of the patients to practice on. The poor were meant to show gratitude, and while hospitalized were less of a health risk, particularly in large towns such as Exeter where many were household living-in servants! It was also whilst they were confined that they formed a captive audience for discipline and sermons. Exeter hospital advertised itself as being 'of the greatest consequence not only for the health & welfare, but also to the religion and morals, of the laborious poor'. There was a busy buzz of activity and moralising in Georgian England!

Chapter 6

Page110 It was the July quarter sessions that Rebecca's case had been waiting for, though she did not know this. No information was passed on to prisoners ever. They were not only treated as but also called 'prisoners' the principle being that 'if a man is very wretched, there is no harm in making him more so!

Page114. The public gallery was always overflowing with the general public at its worst, there to see the public humiliation of whoever was in the dock. Heckling from the gallery was common place and in fact encouraged by the prosecution and the judge. In a petty treason case such as Rebecca's the queues for the public gallery would have started as soon as her trial was announced, usually a couple of days before. Voyeurism was at its worst and sympathy unheard of.

Page 104. Counsel would have had to be paid and Rebecca certainly would not have had the wherewithal to do so therefore it is unlikely that she had a defence counsel, therefore she would have to conduct her own defence. Rebecca would have been given a few days notice of her trial and would have been asked if she wanted to call any character witnesses in her defence. It is unlikely she would have understood what was asked of her, and there is no record of her trial in existence so we do not know whether indeed she did call any. Witnesses for the prosecution however would have been called had she not pleaded guilty. Certainly Mary Jarvis, her accuser, together with other members of the Jarvis family would have been called. Witnesses both for the prosecution and the defence, if there were any, were kept together in a witness room outside the court, and not separately. It is known that the judge and jury on duty that day were Sir Richard Park, Thomas Taylor, Buck Fortesque Esq., John Laroche, James Pitman, John Burridge, and the clerk was George Croke. However the trial transcript from this particular Quarter Session has been missing for some time. Character was a negotiable quality, and a vital part of the evidence both for and against the defendant. Judges regarded 'good' character as good defence and the opposite 'bad' defence. However what was good character to one judge was not good character to another. We shall never know what was said in Rebecca's trial, but we do know she pleaded guilty. We can see this from the pamphlets printed by Elizabeth Bryce accompanying the trial and issued shortly after her Page 107. I quote: (Exeter Public Records Office. Loc. LE 1782/07/29. EG5.)

The Life, Charactre, Confession, and dying Behaviour of REBECCA Downing, burnt at Heavytree, Monday, July 29th 1782, for Poisening her Master, Richard Jarvis. Pr. By Elizabeth Bryce (1782) -1 sheet.

Rebecca Downing, born at East Portlem0uth, Devon, was the illegitimate child of parents, transiently connected by appetite rather than affection, and little caressed by either of them, was committed to the lukewarm tenderness of a parish nurse. Infants thus circumstanced are mostly considered as born but to labour, and little attention is paid to education.

Thus, at 8 years old, Rebeca Downing, totally uninstructed, was by the parish apprenticed to Mr Richard Jarvis of the above place, who commonly employed her in the fields to pick weeds, stones, attend cattle and such-like occupations. Her mental capacity was naturally dull, and surely could not be such improved by these rustic employments. The family consisted only of Mr. Jarvis, his grand-daughter and Rebecca, Having thus from birth been in a state of bondage, servility and ignorance, and now doomed to drudge in solitude, without an equal to converse or recreate with, it cannot surprise, that she should contact a indolent and sulleness of temper, and commit frequent faults in judgement and conduct, sufficient to provoke chastisement from a master advanced to the tedious old age of 70. Her indolence felt labour a misery, chastisement rather begat ill-will than industry, and ignorance and gloom w------ speed the murder of the old man as a ready means of relief.

With this design, in May last, she took a quantity of a liquid preparation of arsenic, wherewith her master washed diseased horses, and put it in the tea-kettle with the water to be boiled fir his and the grand-daughter's breakfast, whose morning beverage was usually parched wheat prepared in the manner of coffee. Of this the young woman drank nearly half a pint and the old man twice as much. Violent vomiting immediately succeeded. The grand-daughter, knowing the girl's sullen temper, and recollecting that in her presence she had the day before discoursed with the old man on the poisonous quality of the above liquor, suspected the mischief and accused the servant of the deed. She denied it; but pressed to prove her innocence by drinking a basin of the beverage, she took little in her mouth and spit it out again on the pretence that it was too hot. On examining the vessel which contained the poisonous preparation, about a pint was found to have been taken. Medical aid was instantly called, but Mr Jarvis died in two days. The girl confessed her guilt to the physician, and assigned a desire to be free of servitude as the motive. She was convicted of petty treason and murder, at the Castle of Exon. Thursday July 25th, and sentenced to be burnt.

During her confinement in goal, she was with much difficulty taught to repeat the Lord's Prayer and part of the Creed; but, being catelyzed, was incapable of fixing a meaning to the words. Being questioned if she had ever heard of a God, she answered, Yes, but as to a Saviour's having been on the earth, she said, she had never heard of any such thing. When questioned as to her notion of a immortal soul being formed in her body and which after death was to enter eternal happiness or misery, she said, she knew not what the question meant, and had never been told anything about a soul. Her mother now lives at in Portlemouth and never visited her after her commitment. She constantly owned her guilt, and said, the thought of poisoning her master suddenly entered her head whilst she drest herself in the morning on which she did it, on recollecting that he had chastised her about a month before. She said she meant no harm to the young woman, nor even in the least thought of her being poisoned, tho she knew she usually breakfasted with the old man. Sometimes a tear fell, but on the whole she seemed more stupefied than grieved by her situation. She suffered in her 16th year.

EXON. Printed by ELIZABETH BRICE, near East Gate.

Page 107. The crime of a servant murdering her master whether by poisoning or otherwise, was Petty Treason by virtue of 25 Edward 111, c. 2, the punishment of which was, prior to the 30 Geo, 111, c, 48 (1790), in the case of a man to be drawn and hanged, and a woman to be draw and burnt.[13]

Page 109. This sort of case, that of petty treason, was considered one of the most major against society, and in this case the sentence for the crime, having been perpetrated by one of the very lowest of orders, a pauper apprentice, was to be used as an example of how to control the lower orders. It is debateable if, had this trial been heard in London, where certainly ideas about the benefit of a death sentence being a deterrent was being debated, whether Rebecca might have been treated more leniently, but Exeter was out in the sticks where life was still fixed in a time warp. Modern ideas of leniency had not filtered down that far from the great metropolis.

Page 117. Had they known she would be condemned to death in such a ghastly way? We should wonder! Court sentences were often predicted and fed to the rabble before they happened. It is almost certain that the broadsheets had predicted her death, though the sentence of burning was certainly more than had been expected. Hanging alone would have been more reasonable considering her age and most would have expected her sentence to have been commuted to transportation, except the timings were all wrong![15] Rebecca was to become one of the victims of this short intermediate period after the transportation of prisoners to America was ended, and before Australia became the home to the pathetic small time criminal of the 18th and 19th century. Time between sentencing and the carrying out of a sentence of death was very short. There was time for appeal, but only if the condemned had money, which for Rebecca was not an option.

Chapter 7
Page 105. Even before they were proved guilty, in the eighteenth century accused people were denied any

rights except the right to rule-bound trial, and pending that they could be imprisoned for months as they waited the next assizes or quarter sessions. Bail was rare and unheard of for any-one who had been accused of committing a murder.

Page 106. Criminal trials of the period were casual and rowdy and over very fast, in fact few trials took more than half an hour, and in most cases only lasted ten minutes.[3] It has been noted that 'a full two thirds of prisoners, on their return from their trials, cannot tell of anything which has passed in the court, not even very frequently, whether they have even been tried'.(Gatrel p. 537)

Page 106. Before the Act of 1790 was passed this was the usual punishment for all sorts of treasons committed by those of the female sex.' It can be noted that Blackstone, referring to old punishments in cases of treason says 'The humanity of the English Nation was authorised by a tacit consent, and almost general mitigation of such parts of the judgements as savour of torture or cruelty: a sledge or hurdle being usually allowed to such traitors as are condemned to be drawn, and there being very few instances (and those accidental or by negligence) of any persons being embowelled, or burned, till previously deprived of sensation by strangling.'

Page 109. According to Elizabeth Bryce, Rebecca was only held in prison till July 29th, thus there were only four days after her trial held on Thursday 25th July, till her execution. This means that the above report was made twelve days later. We know from the jailer's ledger of incoming prisoners that she was brought back to Exeter Prison as a condemned prisoner on the 25th. Prisons were not made for holding prisoners, and those that were condemned were despatched very quickly after their trial in order not to incur more expense to the town. What went through the mind of this poor girl is difficult to imagine during those four days. We know she had a visit from Elizabeth Bryce, and I have summised that she might have had one from her mother, this is only conjecture however. What we do know is that on the day of her execution she appeared to be totally unaware of what was going on around her. There is the strong possibility that she was given either strong beer or gin to numb her brain. This was not uncommon. It is known that upwards of 3000 people watched her being dragged to the place of execution, be strangled and (hopefully dead), then burnt.

Page 115. The Morning Herald of 10th August 1782 also contained an observation by 'C' (name unknown) which claimed Rebecca had shown 'Callous indifference'. He wrote 'This callous indifference was confirmed by an eyewitness of the execution, who told a friend of mine who died of a ripe age a few years since that some boys had climbed to the branch of a tree just opposite the stake the better to view the spectacle; and just before the fatal noose was drawn the branch broke and the boys came down in a heap.; which so tickled the culprit that she burst out laughing.' One can only hope the executioner made sure she was dead before setting fire to the faggots. There is no record to confirm this fact, but is does appear from the above eye witness account that at least she was strangled first, and that she was basically unaware of either her surroundings or of what was going to take place. We can only hope that there was not a gross miscarriage of justice in her fate.

PART 111

Chapter 1

Page 117. It was Mary's mother who was Jarvis's daughter, so one can probably assume that , on marriage, the newly married couple had moved to where her husband lived at first, or even with his parents as often young married children remained in the family house for quite some time before they could afford to take a place of their own. It is surprising that Mary did not remain with her paternal grandparents, though they might not have been alive, which would have explained her being sent to live with her elderly grandfather who was well into his late 60's, an advanced age in the 18th century.

CONCLUSION

Page 130. Between the years from 1775 when the America gained her independence from the British, and they refused to accept any more convicts, and the year 1787 when transportations resumed to Australia, those who would normally have been transported were sent to the prison ships, in this case moored off Plymouth. After the War of Independence in America of 1776, the detrus of society was no longer welcome on those shores. Tasmania was not an option yet. The idea of sending petty criminals to Australia had not been mooted. Consequently what was Britain to do with its criminals? Prison hulks were laid up outside Portsmouth, Southampton and on the Thames, but they were soon filled. Sentencing reflected the need to rid England of its criminal classes for good, so execute where possible was the answer!